EXPLORING THE CLOUDS

Also by John Fraser
and published by
AESOP Modern Fiction:

Animal Tales
The Answer
Behaving Well
Best Friends
Black Masks
Blue Light / Starting Over
The Case
Confessions
Down from the Stars
The Ends of the Earth
Enterprising Women
The Future's Coming Everywhere
Happy Always
Hard Places
An Illusion of Sun
The Magnificent Wurlitzer
Medusa
Military Roads
The Observatory
The Other Shore
People You Will Never Meet
The Red Bird
The Red Tank
Runners
'S'
Short Lives
Sisters
Soft Landing
The Storm
Strangers and Refugees
Thinking Scientifically
Thirty Years
Three Beauties
Tomorrow the Victory
Wayfaring
Wisdom

EXPLORING THE CLOUDS

John Fraser

AESOP Modern Fiction
Oxford

AESOP Modern Fiction
An imprint of AESOP Publications
Martin Noble Editorial / AESOP
28a Abberbury Road, Oxford OX4 4ES, UK
www.aesopbooks.com

First edition published by AESOP Publications

www.johnfraserfiction.com

A catalogue record of this book is
available from the British Library.

First edition 2021, revised 2024

ISBN: 978-1-910301-89-0

CONTENTS

EXPLORING THE CLOUDS

IT'S A SMALL WORLD. I don't have much time to find out all about it.

My despatcher, sponsor, Odette, pulls sprigs of willow from her soft hair, pushes, pulls, at my shoulder.

'Go with God,' she says. We laugh. The park is empty. I suspect we should not be here. She says:

'There's no more first person. That's finished. No more 'garden door closing softly', no more 'the ghost her father's parting gift....' No reminiscences – we all have them. Dull. No quest for justice or an ending – it's all been said. We're waiting. Bring me back – earth, blood, life. Something I can sell, diffuse – in quantities you can't imagine.'

The little waterfall makes foam, that lingers. We turn away. It's all been said.

A SWIFT TRIP TO MEXICO

'I used to be more colourful, Manlio. Now, I'm reflective.'

I talk too much, I confess: there it is.

He too reflects – maybe goes blank, scans the bus as if the voyagers are all his postulants. He says offhand:

'No! You're the same; profligate as a fruitfly. But let's move down – that guy at the end is sick. His eyes are sucked, his nose runs detergent, his trunk sags like a bag of chestnuts. I'm a doctor – I'd tell you what he has, if you could understand.'

We all squeeze away from the dying one, down the bus that bucks and squalls.

*

'Pill or mushroom?' the driver said. 'Don't look up or down. You can't look out....' It's true – each window is a saint, who died for us, left a slim volume, spells you shouldn't try. Transfers block the view – blue, brown and yellow....

Manlio peers at the sick passenger: 'He's in full spate – but he will leave a skeleton that's wonderful. Clean, absolutely white. You, Torsten, what have you decided you will leave?'

'Fossilisation's too long a shot,' I say, as we stop to lay the late guy in a stratum of sphagnum mud. 'It's too protracted for me. Unpredictable too, after those dull years, the millions. I had in mind something more philosophical. Each species, as it peaks and drops, should leave its core idea carved on a redoubt. Indecipherable, perhaps. Who cares?

'For humans – that idea's the discovery of time. They count their years, their seconds. That's their emblem: big time, long and short times. The Big Time. Time's short. As long as it takes. Space time, jail time. Time of the essence, time wasted, time revisited, time spent, time lost. Time's up. Out of time. You've had your time. It's economies. Everything must go, closing down. Sell before you starve.... The base of action and emotion, of sequence and of consequence. Everybody living knows it. Time flies. Time wounds. Wrinkles and dentures, boredom, adultery.

'But how to pass it on? To what? The discovery of what's invisible but gnaws at everything? What you know, remember, what you forget, what you give yourself and don't allow other people? What has time brought us anyway? Extinction, and an heir quite not like us at all, with buggy features, slippery skin?'

'It's true,' says Manlio, not much impressed. 'The dinos thought they were for ever; millipedes don't even need to count. They have abundance of their spares. Extinction and eternity – neither's painful.'

Death: leaves its banal thought. And – this time, it wasn't yours.

I thought Brazil was trees and mountains. Here, it's flat, there's nothing much at all. Green and yellow food: for the cows that we can't see? Or for the humans, staring at us, in ragged clothes?

*

There's people who have 'nothing'. They have what I would throw away. Now, they risk having less. I owe them nothing – nothing's what they have. My history, my country – it doesn't have a relationship, no guilt, blame, a contact even; not with the tiny towns here, people packed in, a puzzle, a coloured cube, blocks built of packing cases, oil drums, stuff that lasts for centuries, black water running down the alleyways – little towns that buzz with what you wouldn't want and people you'd not trust; shushed at night ... slurring troubled syllables. Transactions that are better not....

But – of course, I live in the shadows of illumination: the luminaries, reason and therefore doubt, and disagreement. So – I ask.

*

'Look at me. I have nothing. I have my clothes to sit and stand in. Other people – their nothing is much bigger than what you can see on me – they have families, religions, debts. Some have credits, or projects, or someone on the inside. They must have – or they'd weep all night.

'Arrogance: means you speak of nothing, toss it in the crispy air, bestow it on someone else. You are the only one. Your nothing interests you deeply.

'Try being honest.'

Manlio can't hear. He isn't meant to.

*

'Prison doesn't suit,' says Manlio. 'Not me, not you, Torsten. Here, we have the doorless walls. Then – the poor, the precarious, all around; their gloomy webs. My life's got very small. But you, Torsten, – you have the illusion that you can resist. Be yourself, change everybody. You can't. Ignorant people: they hunt you through a forest of shrouds hung up to dry. They don't even know they're carrying out their orders.'

'That's paranoia, Manlio,' I say: 'And arrogance. The clever ones are there to help the others. I'm not a clever one. I join in, but I know you don't find anything by joining in.

'There is no mystery. There's just to set it out, things are as they are. Thing: as it is.

'It gets harder, harder to go on, and we, the species, must know that failures will accumulate. We despair. Once we might have seemed the victors – now, we know. We are the usual losers. There is no shame involved. How do we lose? What do we do when we have lost? It's not just me who asks; it's millions who didn't calculate the time, the histories, the clockwork, scan the cogs of social life. We calculated families and countries, not the ends of life, and earth.'

A prayer for the guy we're burying? You're joking.

'I'm leaving *now*,' the driver shouts.

'That mud is wonderful,' says Manlio, as we cram back in the bus. 'He's lucky – he'll end up somewhere in a case, a crystal case. Well preserved. Delicate; the bones ... tell what he last ate ... the teeth! Rocks, sedimented ... quartz and fluorspar. He is precious stones.

'Be very careful, Torsten. Sex, debt and work. They drag you in, you can't get out, there is no way. You must betray or rot, if you let them take a hold. Aloof! Stay cool. Watch me! My method works....'

I think – everybody has a method, they all work, not much. There are obstacles: not talked of, but there's distances you can't hear across....

*

There's little worlds, as small as prune stones, and huge insubstantial ones. Zeppelins. In space, worlds circle involuntarily round a star. In our stuffed heads – no star, no circling.

'People talk to you, Torsten,' says Manlio. 'Because you don't know anything. It's attractive. You acquire acquaintances.'

*

This must be Mexico. We get off, and Manlio goes down the travertine steps in the middle of the huge floating square and disappears.

SETTLING ACCOUNTS

'Sakine,' I say. 'I must be decisive. Put order into everything. Us two – I feel we've had everything we could, from each other....'

It's enough. She cries and leaves.

There's time, all afternoon; thin and dry like breadsticks. Nibble at it – there is always more, and stale.

What a jumble she is – a marvel ... all colours, all words, about to pass the frontier into somewhere else.

I call her: 'Sakine! I made an error.... When can you come over?'

There's silence. Relief? Joy?

I ask, 'Is there someone there with you?'

Laughter and snorting. 'I'm tied up right now,' she says.

I don't see her again.

PARTY-GOING, ORGY-HOPING

Theme parties – they're not me. It's wrong: in the forest, you dance for food or rain or fire. This here's for thoughtless well-off guys. A muff party – already on the edge of naughtiness, a slang, a double weighting – it rests on bodies you desire to touch – your own, or someone else's. But, you can't – the well-informed wear muffs of fur, of all the species we set out to beat, exterminate, the big beasts, watchful or opportunist, slinking or stalking, the felines, hyenas, even scales: the pangolins and dragons.

Do we wear handcuffs too? They say you can't run with hands cuffed in front – it's not quite true, but it's the touch of cognoscenti, of cons, to say so. I hate these occasions, fake erotic, all fixed beforehand. Some procurer or procurator hides the grasses and the infiltrated, the willing and the curious ... then they whoop, spring out.... Naked from the cake.

They are not for me, you neither. You don't go to jail for crimes we all deplore, fiddling with your peers – you'll have been framed, you'll say, but neither do you find paradise, an eternal partner, in other people. Forget it. They don't exist. Anyone who climbed the hill and stole the mysteries won't share them, not with you, for sure.

'Are you still with Sakine?' asks Odette. 'And how was your long trip? What did you bring back for me? Even nothing, if I can make it a philosophy ... a rule for living over here....'

'It was shells and feathers,' I invent. 'The customs took it off me.'

'I'd love to cuddle you, Torsten,' she invents, 'but there's some game you have to play here so's to get a drink, as we're muff-cuffed.

'Kiss? There's a risk. The easy way is "quit", and "let's find a bar". Here, the partying is stress, with consequences that stop you doing almost anything. It's a new experience, enriching, they say – but I hate education, as I'm sure you do, my dear.'

It's all show. 'It's all Poe,' says Odette. 'Ogres and threats. Nothing has changed. We're fragile animals, taking more than our share of room. Bullying. Making bangs and concrete. We must be very very careful. Do not touch. Not me, not anything. If you want a drink....'

'There's no one to give it to you,' I say, and we laugh as we run down flights of stairs, both fearing elevators.

*

'Find a sailor's bar!' says Odette. 'A crew is like an orchestra – there's shovelling the coal, and polishing the figurehead, cleaning out the crow's nest and the bilge....' We laugh some more. I've been on Odette's ships, the cruises not a bit like symphonies. Mutinies and discords.

'Come now, Torsten,' says Odette. 'Did you discover riches? A destination? Where's my profit?'

'People, living out their time. Knowing nothing more than that,' I say. 'Lifers. That was my find.'

She's cold. 'I collect occasions,' she tells me, as if that's understandable. 'The people here – they'd love a ritual. Instead, they get a puzzle, hope it leads to sex. If I wrote things down, it would be a tell-tale: a tall tale of sex anticipated, fantasised. Everyone's a john, hoping to buy orgasms. And who is selling them?'

Her good feature is the hair: she's wily, one of the last to keep some money, think of sales and voyages. The rest gave up – catastrophe comes regular when you're doing well.

She's maturing; likes to have a squad, young guys, no sex.

*

I found nothing on my trip. I lost Manlio down the underground. Nothing new except what was there before. Going downhill fast isn't finding a new start.

'So,' she says. 'Nothing useful. Nothing to sell, to show, to share, to dig up and export?'

'I'm an agent, Odette,' I say. 'There's millions like. I found wisdom, but if you had the patience, you'd see I took it with me. It can't be monetised, commercialised. What do you want of me? I'm not good at partying ... I helped bury strangers, that is all.'

'Lapis,' she says. 'Lapis lazuli from Badakhshan. Show me how it got to Africa. Then – gold is the glue, eternally, it holds the people in a nest, all hungry. The rest – politics, religion, relatives, all that stuff – pushes them apart. Gold – the great conductor. Map it for me, Torsten!'

'It's a long long way,' I say. 'Afghanistan to Mali. Did they use the blue? They have gold – Lobe, Bambuk, Bure – do you think they paid for ultramarine, the lapis, with their gold?'

'I've no idea,' she says. 'Savannah elephants with big lovely tusks – the furniture, with ivory insets ... in Begram. Lapis for the paint, the manuscripts.... Gao, Timbuktu,

Tadmekka. The past, Torsten – we have to dig in it, the places that were once. Link it all up, connect it, make a story, dig up a tablet where it's all incised. Make me famous for an hour.'

'All guesses, Odette. Boutique fantasy,' I say. 'It's your obsession. Fake scholarship, and clients ignorant of everything except themselves. And with tales of how once, long since, their one world, their gold, could tie it all, the humankind, together.'

'It may be so,' she says. 'Once, only some experts and eccentric guys thought about the future. Now – everybody has ideas. How frightening it is, until the end. Not having kids. No one to share your fear, your dread, inherit it.

'And now – everybody's mad about sex and moving round, finding a lair and quitting the next day. Lifting weights, gorging on steroids....'

'It wasn't gold, Odette,' I say. 'That tied it all. Camels. They did the slog.'

'I thought we'd all have sex,' she says. 'This evening, it was all set up. And then the rules. Another game that stops you doing what you must, and so you find a way to cheat, and it's not good. It doesn't satisfy.'

'Manlio,' I say. 'He was an agent too, like me. He bought for you. He's talented, but ran away.'

'I thought you'd like him, but he got frustrated with you,' Odette says. 'The bus ... stuffy. He's not an agent. He was a trader, trading the wrong stuff. He did bad. Really, quite bad.'

'Honestly, Odette, I found nothing that would interest you,' I say. 'No clients – not to travel, invest, or buy. There's nothing for sale: it's all been contracted, all toughed up. Nothing ephemeral, nothing inventive.'

'It was just bus fares, Torsten,' Odette says, moving away. 'I thought it helped, giving you some cash. You know I love you. I depend on you and your approval.'

'There was no change, Odette,' I say. 'Not a cent. I spent it all.'

It isn't true.

I go on, 'I don't owe you. Not money, I mean. There's a chance, though: the movies. There's locations – lots and lots, but flat. No animals. Just cows.'

She twists around, away. 'There's a photographer, Elise,' she says, proud and apologising. 'She's with me these days – photos from video games – imaginary landscapes.'

'Is it serious?' I ask.

'Oh no,' says Odette. 'People are gross. All titillation, then they want it real. These parties – a heap. Nothing can happen – then it all does. It's terrifying. That's why you go.'

We think about that.

'Even in Africa,' she says. 'Choreography. All planned, the song and dance. Academies for everything. Changing life utterly. It runs through society – a silver knife.'

'I don't follow, Odette,' I say. 'I've only been away two months.'

'For ever,' she says, and laughs. 'Anyway – Brazil doesn't join on to Mexico. You missed out countries, Torsten.'

'I guess I was asleep,' I say.

'Like Sudan is next to Cameroon?' she asks. 'You, sleeping on a sack of lapis.'

'Leave it, Odette,' I say. 'Africa's been taken. Most everywhere is. Asia's been contracted. Europe's depressing. Think of selling ideas, not objects.'

'I think of selling bodies,' Odette says. 'But you must not. Except – it's what happens. By the hour. You must get used to danger, or you'll find life's very hard.'

'It's regression,' I say. 'People explode, regret – then bang!'

'Don't poke into other lives. Get it out. Curiosity's not enjoyable, not your fantasy, or anyone's. Share it, let it happen, get over it,' she says.

'Elise – how is she?' I ask.

I think of Odette a lot. Even in fantasy, she's quite inert. She reflects:

'Elise has a touch of porphyry – that illness all the royals have. She's wild. Out of focus.'

ELISE: THE IMAGE OF REALITY

Odette's my income. I am hers. If I'm not sent off to find a line to buy – she suffers.

There's Elise, in pyjamas, taking snaps – into a small box, full of cut-out shapes. 'We are all grovelling,' she says. 'Even nudes are out – no one takes exercise, they explode, the models – it's like snapping polenta someone's dropped.'

'Odette is looking good,' I say. That's my hook.

'She's babying up,' Elise says, sharp. 'It's early onset. Losing your mind, does good things for skin. Doesn't know me, who I am.'

'I don't either,' I say. 'Maybe it's so – Odette's older than us two together, but she's spry.'

'That is a word,' says Elise. 'Well chosen, Torsten. Of course! You buy for her.... Buy cheap, sell cheaper – that is how it's done. The giants, they do that. Make rings round everyone – gold rings.'

'Her clients want history and exotics, but the good stuff is just crumbled bits, the rest is fake,' I say.

'Oh yes?' Elise says, sniffily. 'You guys are dealing on the side – if you were croupiers, the punters would grill your livers for their tea.'

'It's the electronics,' I say. 'Collecting has changed key. You have everything before you now: treasure's complete, untouchable on your screen. So, what's to sell?'

Elise grins at me. There must be something big with Odette. She grins wider, her skull like the rock crystal ones they wanted me to buy in Tenayuca. 'Whaddya think?' she asks, tapping an incisor. 'Odette's gift.'

'Heroin teeth?' I am surprised.

'They're gems, drilled in,' Elise says. 'Love tokens. Some didn't take, and some were dicey. It's a conversation point.'

'It's a unique idea,' I say. 'It's Odette's business, of course.'

I peer closely at the box she's snapping – 'It's a toy theatre,' she says. 'You make the little houses and bandits get posted on and run about and *ados* in the bedroom spend hours shooting them .... For you, it's finick: ships in bottles, matchstick Notre Dames....'

I'm sorry for her. All the money she must make!

'All that matters is the artist,' Elise says, forcefully. 'These materials, the public – shit! It's compulsory. It's because we're animals with bodies. All that matters is myself. Without me – nothing. The creator, me, the artist. That's what the teeth show, Torsten. Think cathedrals – the light comes through the painted glass, material. That's religion. That is God.'

'I'm partly with you, Elise,' I say. 'You must get down to lower levels; millions will buy, not even think of you. But – it's the teeth. You'd be an artist even if you'd dentures. Gums. The artist is afflatus, not celebrity. Rose is a rose, it can be no other. Formaldehyde the hand or slice the brain – you'll not find any secret.'

'There is none, Torsten,' Elise says. 'Secrets are mistakes. The camera is a tool for dullards. What I see is much much more than you can print. The image is just itself, it's not *of* anything. It is for sale. I'm not.'

'I didn't see you at the party,' I say. 'It seems a lot of fuss to get us drunk, have intercourse....'

'Fuss,' she says. 'You're on the right track. Culture. Civilisation.'

'Ah,' I say. 'I understand. It's not the content – it's the form! You're retained here by Odette to take the picture – of our accomplishment. Like, I was to bring back something – an indication – of how we've plodded on.... Those empires in the desert, the Sahel, the empty quarter, Mongols and Manchus, the Turkic nomads. Devastating, building what we had in mind, if mind we had ... Gurdjieff.... Over and over, starting up and sacrificing, digging, depleting, exporting, trafficking – what were we after? What has it made, accumulated – left? And you were there to make the video record.

'*I* was to do the trade. The bus stopped to let us pee in Honduras. My gaze – it was a threat, a bad bargain. I give money and take you and your culture. What will it be? Do I buy clay figurines? An ocarina? Spit on some sores?'

She doesn't speak. Her teeth flash riches – little kids bringing the stones up from muddy shafts, laid at the feet of power, sold on, bought with a card, gifted, paid as ransom or as tribute, locked in a box....

'Odette has foresight,' Elise says. 'It's us that must flesh out the vision.... You're a prophet, Torsten. We all are. Harassing others so we can preen ourselves. Everyone who sees my pics owes me more than they will ever earn by selling themselves or their companions.'

*

'You know, Torsten,' Odette says, 'I'm not an ecologist. Once I was, like everyone – but everything has gone too far. Let's eat the animals we want, drive our buggies over Madagascar ... what the hell! But did you draw conclusions on your trip...?'

'Oh, I'm with you,' I say. 'There is no going back. There's dams and hollowed mounds, excavations, mines, all flat and dry. Deserts ready to be born. Brazil shows us – it's all over. finished.

'An epitaph? See if there's a message we could leave.... A simple warning, mea culpa, possibly....'

'No no,' she says. 'No messages no one will read. Encapsulate the best we were in your good puffed-up life. And let me sell, or we shan't eat, and you won't get to travel, seek out the curious, the intelligent....'

'You mean,' I say, 'you won't sell stuff in your boutiques: only people. Sages, gurus, gardeners and warriors....'

'Something like that,' she says. 'Elise is looking out for visuals.'

'Elise is stout, like Cortès,' I say. 'She looks out on nothing less than worlds. But – species. It's a neutral term, and so am I. I don't care if the species falls, divided or united. No care, no sweat. Not at all.

'I'll help buy stuff, and help your trade. But – about the accomplishment, the ultimate – I do not care. No, not at all.'

'Then you're not trustworthy,' she says, shocked, shaken – 'Something must be left. A carving – for the headstone. A story – it must have an end. Or else! Remember, "*vieux pays merveilleux des contes de nourrice*" ... that wonderful fairy-tale world – it's ours, Torsten: our hills, our continents.'

'No, Odette, it's not ours. "*We* belong to *it*,"' I say. 'We're chips of shale, of pyrites, drops of gutta percha. We can't be otherwise. That is the end you get, Odette. No story, unless you make one up.'

'Then, Torsten,' she says. 'You're not in my dependence. Your life is bloat.'

'You're desperate, Odette,' I say. 'Open to anything. If you thought you could gain time, you'd back up a regime, find one – however horrible, degenerate, regressive. Aristotle said those are the murderous shades of earlier valid ones: they're fallen hopes....

'You're indiscriminating. It's over, Odette: the end's no longer nigh, it's written on the wall.'

*

We separate in anger.

*

Elise says to me, 'I bet you were awake in your journey, more than you would want to tell.'

'We should start a corporation, Elise,' I say, suddenly enlightened. 'That way you can do anything. Rule, give charity, say what you please, hoard and spend, be mysterious, be embarrassing.

'Give people room to plot, display themselves, suspect each other. Proclaim the truth, so's you can tell your lies in anonymity....'

'Too late, Torsten,' says Elise, flashing her teeth. 'It's all been done – and you, the partying moralist, must know it!'

'Not moralism, Elise,' I say, peering past her grin, down, along, her small exciting body. 'I'm timid, that's all.'

*

'I feel I'm on the wrong side, Elise,' I say. 'But I don't know who's with me and what we'd do. I think: – my side – we'd lose, if we've not already lost ... what? A battle? A war? Alliances?'

'And does it hurt, Torsten?' she asks, gentle pushing my face, my gaze, away. 'You're invasive – even with advice. Corporation? Profits galore, and domination? Yes, my dear, you're drinking the dragon's brew – if you don't spit it out in flame, it'll burn you up. Me? If I can't dodge hot breath, I let it hit my fireproof shell.

'I need no one, stand for nothing. True, I'm for sale, but I'm worth more than whatever you might have.'

'Wars,' I say. 'Humans are very good at winning and at losing them. The organisation is immense, the aims, the mobilisations: this is their real antlike prowess ... enormous numbers, each unit pared down to something entirely new and uniform: bored, terrible, obedient and aggressive. I fear them, Elise. They do what I don't want, but they're Creation.'

'No,' Elise interrupts. 'Not the way you want. Not any way, because you don't know what you want.... Because what you have in front of you, is what there is: and it is what you do not want.... Can't manage. You're stuck. If you can't hold a camera still – you could try sculpture. A chain saw? Swing and twirl!'

'That's a crap idea, Elise,' I say.

She's a joker....

'Or, you could organise a war that you will lose,' she goes on. 'Or maybe you've already done that? Guys who die in losing wars – I wonder how they feel compared to guys who die but in the end, theirs is the winning side.'

'I know all that,' I say. 'It's what you do at school – before you are conscripted. Then, you know no result is up to you.'

'Odette wants you to be useful,' Elise says. 'That should be in your grasp. The rest is bullying poor countries – or ... hard work like you're not good at doing.'

'It's good you know everything, Elise,' I say. 'But bad I can't do photography.'

She's not very articulate: I tell her so; she smiles.

*

'This box,' she says, 'is Persepolis. You can see it's about to be destroyed – the gunfire! The liberators, running over the grey sand.... God the General's chasing the Padishah in tall brass boots – the same He wears in the theatre of Marcellus ... playing the Avenger, Liberator. Eternal Roman soldier. He knocks them down, empires. Those who'd leap up to confront Him – down they go – spares, strikes and gutterballs....

'Are you clothed, Torsten, for when you ride into the big Mafia cities where you'll do business and break the tables of the infidels?'

'I'd never thought,' I say, 'there'd be a question of the right clothes.'

'It's critical when you're naked, like you are now,' she says. 'Having been everywhere and thought every thought available in your language – you monoglot! – you who hide behind your cataract, the water curtain, you who live alone and lonely in your own time ... purblind, unlettered, decaying, flaking out ... how will you see the light, the panorama, when it opens up to you, to us ...? Your blotchy body, bossed with gobs of fat and dying skin – forget the clothes you hide it with – you're naked, going blind and deaf and breathless, impotent, and creaking like a stable door....'

I'm in her light-box, her camera obscura – another bandit panting over her, another screw....

'I know,' I say. 'I'm in good form. Being on the mark requires a solitude. Being here and not there, not somewhere else.... So, what can I do? What's my next scene, what is my line?'

And Elise says, 'I can't enlighten, Torsten: I'm in the same web as you. But I snap! I'm here! I can be nowhere else! And yet – I travel, I make voyages. I can go anywhere, and yet, and yet – I do not move!'

'Perhaps we all shall see everything,' I say, seeing some small light. 'And penetrate. You need a tool, pocket-ready, that lets you into all the other rooms.'

'That's right,' Elise says. 'A mongolfier! Drifting over and above.... An onion – makes you cry, shaped like a grenade.... A marvel. No wings: it is the voice of God.'

'It's not that, not at all,' I say, but she is putting on ballooning clothes. 'Helmets!' she says. 'We shall need our helmets....'

*

Odette hears the shouts. ‘You young ones, sitting round all day, you, Torsten, dreaming of somehow getting into dear Elise – at least, into her scene.... And what do you want, Elise? The rhetoric of being here and also there – bilocation doesn’t satisfy....’

I say, ‘Odette – I sit here, and I fret.’

‘Quick,’ she says. ‘My ballooning clothes, my veil. Inflate! It’s like old times....’

‘It *is* old times,’ says Elise. ‘My cameras won’t work, we’re limited to eyes.’

UP AND DOWN IN A BALLOON

Up, up we go, through the stratum of fog and dust. Light! – 'There's Verdun!' says Odette. 'Smell! The cordite ... gas, corruption. Quick, quick ... away!'

'And there's Marcello,' says Elise, waving, pointing down – much excited and intrigued – 'God! Down there, just lounging.' She calls out – 'Ciao, Marcello! Coooee! Ciao!'

'I'm sure,' I say. 'God was an actor in the Theatre of Marcellus, and so was Mastroianni. The one big God – sees off the rest, the pantheon, the demis and the nymphs....'

'Of course,' says Odette, 'humans took over from them – alive, dead, and probably indeterminate – unseen, not quite alive, not dead. They've all become related, gods and humans. Like watercolour, it all blurs. Everyone is born a child: – where do the parents go? The sages on their rockers, minding the goats ... where did they end up?

'It makes you cry.... Sex.... What a waste, all disappearing as soon as it takes form. And here is Crete! All liars there.... And Egypt, realm of death.... Then the rift, the fire beneath, remember and beware, we're living on a brazier that shakes us in the night.... That's where the rastas go to die, Torsten, you're black so you should know – we've all been slaves and so we'll be the only ones that can be freed....'

And on she talks, we fly, higher than the white birds, then into flocks of black – the cold ones going south; the hot ones north.... Elise talks on – the gods, the movies, 'yet – it moves....'

It's green and yellow. We discount the sea.

'Don't look down, Elsie,' I say. 'They're all dead down there – taking their pics – it doesn't do a thing for them....'

There is no motor driving everything. Just shouts – of despair and 'Goal!' It's all to do with banks, those engines we can't see.

'Down, down!' I say, and Odette looks up 'Voluntary descent' in the pamphlet of instructions, and she says, 'We're weightless! We'll just go up and up, until we disappear....'

'It's all too random,' says Elise. 'It's bits of territory, not making any sense, the rivers dawdle, people make roads to move the trees they cut and then don't use the roads....'

'Oh, paradox,' Odette says, puffing at the flame, the gas. 'Nothing makes its sense unless you start with sense....'

'That isn't all,' I say. 'We see the humans clearing space, it isn't sure what for.... The Martians think we're making landing fields – for them. They can't see money moving up and down, like photosynthesis in stalks of greenbacks, stuff that's tiny from far off but closer to, it's life....'

*

With our brazen helmets, the basket pluming ever higher: – we are Minerva, Mercury and Venus. An apotheosis. Odette throws the instructions down in rage – down the booklet spins, down, down, a scripture from the heavens....

'Don't land,' says Elise, terrified. 'I hate adulation. Worship would destroy all I have lived for....'

Odette laughs. 'The booklet said: "Voluntary descent's reserved, only for Orpheus: involuntary descent ... requires your spiritual advisor...."'

Our laughter adds to the mystery as we sail, float, drift, higher and higher till our khaki canopy blends with the clouds over the Hindu Kush: the warning. The challenge. Killer of Indians. Or misunderstanding? Don't trust the names.... Nature. We're in it, over it – it can't be trusted. Where does that leave us? Mountains – they lure you on, like rivers – they call out to be crossed. Don't cross humans though ... they're dangerous.

'Here's Badakhshan, Odette,' I say, as we cross over. 'Once prosperous, now poor. It goes that way. If we land, we'll see if there's lapis, if they'll send to Africa....'

'Onward, Torsten. No time for scholarly hypotheses.... There's the dear Amu, river of dreams. Siberia, then China, the circuit's quickly done,' says Odette. 'This is not the way, I fear, to find out anything. The perfect view is only had when you're on someone's back. Alas, there's always fuss to take a camel on a plane, and even worse, through customs where they robbed you, Torsten, so you say, of my rich merchandise....'

*

No one forgets, not ever, nothing, it's all there, poised: the bucket – ice water – balanced on the door, as you enter on the stage, rouged and farded, down it comes. It always does. Laughter, applause ... and curtains.

*

'However high we go, however small the people and the places are, however unlike ourselves we must appear,' Odette says. 'Take note. There are some places that should never disappear ... places always ending bad, never a decent shaking of the bag. Let's give them their happy day.'

'It's not like that,' I say. 'It doesn't come in good and bad, and parts deserving better....'

'It's the Congo,' Odette says. 'The Congolese – they have a continent, a chest of treasures and of curiosities: it's terrible, Torsten, the history ... on and on, more terrible....'

'Histories are like that, Odette,' I say. 'It isn't possible to live with any of them, the pasts and futures ... help me out, Elise, you have perspectives I can't conceive....'

'No, no, Torsten,' Elise says. 'Don't bring me into that. Do what you can, conjure a context for whatever you can scheme – it isn't me, it isn't mine. What is awful, what is incomplete – everything, that is, that ever was – is finished. Can't be undone, or re-done. If you lament, you alone can hear; the judgment is of you, and only you. You're never punished, no one ever is, or not enough. Forget it, little soldier, be brave and bold, and if you aren't, it won't affect your fate or anyone's a little bit....'

*

'We ought to land,' I say, but Elise says, 'No, no! It's images, not second homes we seek – on, on until....'

'There's no "until",' Odette says. 'The images, they never stop, they cannot be turned off – until you're blind they come into your head across your eyes, and some are permanently filed, and even when you cannot see, they come in through your ears and nose – rivers, floods of happenstance; and each one means that experience and your pale moralism are separate, indifferent, deaf to each other, until you age, and ethics flickers out and there is more and more of pictures till you conclude, and they – they never ever will.'

'Then there's no project,' says Elise. 'Only to switch off reality.'

*

'Have we seen everything?' Odette asks, not responding to Elise. Our fuel's exhausted, our breath whistles to its end, the wind drops and so do we. Wherever we have landed, it is far, far from where we hoped to be.

*

'Reality's supposed to be the same all over,' says Elise. 'Yet we artists are supposed to make it different, each time we seize it by its long twisted horn.'

'It's the same with humankind,' says Odette. 'We're not supposed to discriminate, although it's always different and always changing – and yet we see it as a stable thing.... What's your view, Torsten?'

'Repetition,' I say. 'I feel it keenly. Quantity. You're always collecting numbers – selling things, doing many things, meeting people, deciding not to relate to some. To many. To almost everyone. And repeating yourself – it's supposed to be a good: it means consistency.

'Order – getting up each day, putting on your clothes, same way, your own day's gender, all the strategic duds. And yet, apart from us being boring, void of interest and substance – we repeat; we march, we copy, we procreate: chips off old blocks. Maybe we should concentrate on being different: unpredictable, original. "Always original." Aha! there you are, fallen in the elephant trap. Being original, always the same. That "always" – a chimera!'

TURNABOUT

'What we saw from the balloon,' Odette says, 'was most disturbing. The scrabble to destroy, rich places much impoverished, the newly rich expecting that exploitation will shortly make them poor. It's all as we've been told. And, much as you are both my loves – Elise and Torsten – do I look to you for help? For what? Rewrite the history of our kind? Another philosophy some studious type excogitates, and makes a stir, disturbs, then it's remaindered with the rest?

'The lesson of the species, grandeur and retribution – a message that's definitive? Neither of you is up to that. It's words and sitting round, going to parties that you like, going on journeys for your inspirations, bringing back nothing at all that's visible, only your sweet familiar heads and scoured-out credit cards....'

'Odette!' Elise shouts. 'The project! The accomplishment, however flawed and incomplete, that humans leave behind – you would abandon that? No stele, and no capsule, no stony trunk, an emblem of a power despoiled, abandoned in the sand...?'

'And me,' I ask. 'The time spent on the bus ... no resource except my copy, greasy, dog-eared, learned by heart and soul – "What is to be Done?" *Chto delat'*?'

'I think she means,' Elise says, 'we might as well be robbers and do fraud, have kids and buy them privilege when we have satisfied ourselves....'

'I shan't prescribe,' says Odette, wiping away some tears. 'Do what you're best at, what comes naturally.... You, Torsten, would learn much from Manlio, who you'd let slip away....'

*

'We can start being bad when I get some money I am owed,' says Elise, curling up on me. 'Do you have a special place where you can hallucinate?'

I'm surprised, even embarrassed. They don't ask it, you don't tell. 'I had hangovers,' Elise goes on. 'Remembering what I'd done. Then, blackouts. They were best. Everything had gone. I could draw directly on the inside of my skull. The prompt lines – they had been rubbed out.'

'What are you afraid of, Elise?' I ask.

'The things that are there, where you left them,' she says. 'What a question!'

'Who owes you money?' I ask Elise. 'What for?'

'If they don't pay you,' she says. 'It sounds like whimsy: a confession.'

'Flowers? Birds?' I ask. 'They're free, but once in the economy, as absences, they ruin you. There's no deal there – they are indifferent. No one pays for what is free, but it costs the earth.'

'That's sharp, Torsten. Not like you. Well done,' she says.

'It'll be delicate,' I say. 'The asking. Pay back. You have to reassure them they're not bad, but you are prepared to be.'

'I think of the reeds,' she says. 'Whispering – "you must weep, weep", *weinen, weinen soll.* It's a terrible hoax, Torsten. Go along with it, or rebel – it's the same. Always the moon, on cloudback. Soft Vienna nights, after the rain, the emperor....'

'You're not that old, surely,' I say, lightening it up, but also fearful.

'It's all written in us,' she says solemnly. 'The numbers on our skin, the stock of wine jars. Retsina – ugh!'

'I hope it's a lot of cash,' I say.

'It's the person,' she says. 'Making a monkey of you, as if monkeys aren't good at sums.'

'Manlio,' I say. 'He should tell us how to be wise, breaking laws.'

'Yes,' Elise says brightly. 'You need to be expert, know most things, to make toughness, bullying, a career.

'Cloths on the canteen tables. That's what shows you can collect your debts. Crime – it's costly, you have to live up to it – no cold spaghetti in paper bags.'

'If it's a bother, let's forget it,' I say.

'No,' she says. 'It makes me angry. The world runs on paying back – light and dark, soil and sand, war and peace. Slap and tickle.'

'We'll get instruction,' I say, 'from Manlio. The crime, or whatever his word for justice is.'

'I've realised,' says Elise, 'about Odette. They didn't use lapis in Timbuktu. The ivory in Begram came from Indian elephants.'

'What a comedown!' I say. 'Of course! We were conjured away on a hypothesis.'

'As for you, Torsten,' she says, 'you're not ready to make love with me.'

'It hadn't occurred to me,' I say. 'I'm sure you're right about that, like about the elephants.'

THE TREE OF LIFE

Eventually, we track down Manlio. 'I'm a doctor,' he says, 'and none of you is sick. What do you want of me? A snake artist, a drummer – those are more your line.'

'My best friend, Elodie,' Elise says, 'I paid her for a tree of life. That, I could photograph. But she gave up – except she won't give up the cash.'

'This is an awful task,' says Manlio. 'Violence and reason; both are imminent, in tandem, or by one and one.'

He's aged, since we last met. Curing or burying – for the expert, they both exact a toll....

'People die, in hunts like this,' he says. 'A doctor can't to anything – a fall from height, a sewer plugged, a cave-in, flame-out.... Don't bother calling me.'

'It's not to do with trees or lives,' says Elise. 'To be autonomous of Odette ... that's the first step. Freedom. You must have read – to be real bad requires a capital: without a creditor....'

He laughs. 'At school, they must have told you – all money, of any kind, converted into materials, such as a zebu or a yak, gold, platinum or lead, struck up or bullion – it all connects. It's all one, convertible, transportable, you kill for it and die for it, it is a web, and spiders are the millions of us trying to weave their square of silken trap, and keep their money tied, secure, within the frame and yet divorced from all the rest.' He concludes, solemnly, 'There is no autonomy with cash.'

'I lived years of sacrifice,' says Elise. 'I'm the animal who sacrifices herself: – usually the beast's the victim, the doe whose tongue goes in the brazier with the other tongues – the god enjoys them, so they say. A real connoisseur, that god – nourished and appeased, just by the smell of roasting.'

'Of burning,' says Manlio. 'Sacrifice needs a god, a worshipper. If you don't have both, it's all a waste.'

'Oh,' says Elise. 'I've burned, and never been consumed. Elodie knows all about the pyre. She sets you on it, and you twist up there. It's a pleasure so extreme it leaves you devoted ... a madness, a psychosis, over and over, always the same, like Tibetans crawling round the sacred mount. A ritual on stones and clay. Clothes, flesh, shredded as you follow the scarred feet ... of the Tibetan crawling round in front of you....'

'Suppose,' I say, 'that what is obvious is also true. Let's view the case.

'Elodie – she has a net. She throws it, light as clouds, and there you are again. The ram, caught in the thicket. It means a special kind of hunt, no fanfares, and no stirrup cups. And if she doesn't like you? What's the snag? It's all the same, love, hate, or just indifference. You're dragged back from your thin existence – a captive. Or – sometimes, you're not. You're spared, by special messenger. It's chance, fortune. Elodie – she doesn't know if you're the rebel or the acolyte, and so – it doesn't matter much which you might think you are. She plays you as you come. Sacrifice? – it's never like you say. Propitiation, favours – don't be misled. Wishes granted always go sour, they come to you already on the turn.

'Elodie – I'm sure she has a body – supple as a sack of billiard cues – exciting, androgyne. All things to you, to all of us. Better to imagine? Better a context that won't repeat: an afternoon; the first time. She's always ready, on the stage, the weather's motionless – and so you think you can direct, repeat the scene, excitement – but, by definition – the starting over's gone and unrepeatable. But – it's the cult – the sacrifice, you must repeat, use the same formula, remember the gestures, the strokes, the sallies, the retreats.... There's conquest and delight, or you'd not participate. Those are just shadows, though: what's always fresh is your acceptance, to act as sacrifice. That is the ceremony....'

'Go get the money,' Manlio says. 'She'll bind you, or she'll let you go. We'll see.'

'How are you involved, then, Manlio?' I ask.

'You can guess that, Torsten,' Manlio says. 'I lay out the dead, that's all. What can't go forward – I make sure it's put away, out of sight.'

THE PACIFIC

She lives high up on a hill that overlooks the sea – as if the hill is made of houses, tiny houses, russet and blue, blue and russet.

'You're back,' says Elodie, ignoring me and Manlio, holding the length of Elise's arm and pressing it against herself. 'For how long are you here this time?'

Quite hard, tense, she sounds.

There's an old framed poster on her wall: a Baader-Meinhoff face. 'Their wars, our war; always, everywhere,' it says.

It's what I think, but that's a thought that gets you into trouble. I'm drawn to Elodie, she's indifferent to me, absolutely, always. She quite likes Manlio, who has some presence I suppose.

This is a house where you can see at once – there's no money here; not much joking, no fooling round.

*

She has no part, no role, it seems, in the story Elise has spun around her. There's much fear here – both women, afraid of different things: Elise fears consequences, fears the antics of her mind and body. Elodie fears history and falling out of it, no trace, and lots of pain.

Elise and Elodie – their features are different, the rest, the meagre bodies, could have been pressed out from moulds, identical. They stand close, and as Manlio and I move awkwardly around the little room, they seem, from some angles, to be one. There's no room for a decent tree of life – maybe there's a space above the ceiling with a trap. A real tree? A sketch: maybe in oils ... an idea, cuttings, seeds ... kept in an old pot for pills. Here, there's the one room for everything, living, sleeping, eating. Being frightened, plotting, waiting for the cops. I feel Elodie doesn't eat a lot.

Outside there's dogs, tiny children, and then grey sea for ever.

'The fascism here is grey, like the sea, like the uniforms,' says Eloide. 'Eternal. You go; it stays.'

*

'We can send out for food,' says Elodie. 'Before you go. Italian?'

She means pizza. Standing round. Who will get to stay? There's one chair, like in the game. For the winner, or for the prisoner? Lots of us. No music, though.

'Who's this?' asks Elodie, pointing at Manlio. 'What's he doing here?'

'There was money involved, I think,' he says, doubt growing with each word.

This space – it's her, we're stood inside her head. There's the tree of life – it must be a dwarf, storm-wracked, a bonsai: – strong? Who knows.

'Any money – it's been spent,' says Elodie. 'What did you expect?'

'You shouldn't take and spend,' Elise says. 'Not doing what it's for. It's not that the work you do won't please me, or the use I make of it isn't pleasing to you or anyone. It's money paid by me to you for work not done. It is suspended,' and she waves around the little room as if there is potential not realised, a spectral safe, a bag of cash deflating like a lung.... 'Unresolved. A fragment....'

'There's nothing here,' says Manlio: 'Elise, why did we come?'

'Why are you here?' asks Elodie, looking for some way to chase off Manlio. 'To check on me, Elise? See if I was here alone? Stay with me, take me away? Being a whore – that brings money here, it's all there is – was that the trail?'

She's frantic now, poor Elodie, and Elise ... why's she here, bringing foreigners ... the neighbours call the cops for much much less....

'Come away,' Elise takes Elodie's thin arm and pulls. Elodie stands firm. 'Forget the politics. It isn't you, you won't kill them but they'll kill you.'

'You haven't understood, Elise,' says Elodie. 'Money and death – you've invented the money, and you fear the death. You bring it with you, it's the exchange, a gift you think will bring you – something. Riches, reputation, even me. I am the witness – they will bring death. Not me, I don't bring anything.

'When you left, you took the tree of life – so small, maybe you didn't even see....'

'The customs, everywhere,' I say, 'are very strict about live plants....' It's true, but I'm ignored. And is there love here, monetised? A sacrifice, prepared here, in this cage?

'I can't leave,' says Elodie. 'I would be caught. Besides – who wants me?'

'Do you want martyrdom, my dear?' Elise asks. She seems exasperated. 'Martyrs must be unknown, and unrecorded. Then, if you win, your side, that is: the dead are totted up. And that is it! Unloved, unknown, until you die, and then you wait, maybe for ever. For a summing up of sacrifice. But sacrifice is self-denial. You throw yourself away in order.... Well, for what? To have that question asked for ever on your bones – why? What for? What is accomplished, what prophecy...? Where is that tree of life? Where is your life?

'A victim, foretold, forewarned. If it's love you want, you must go out, face the world – and let's pretend the land is bigger than the sea, that heaves, restless, monotonous to no horizons, unpopulated – land's where love is, if there is love at all. And if you grasp its slippery tail, as it goes scuttering – Oh Elodie! – it's quicksilver, shapeshifting, moments of ease and then the waiting, doubt, you slide, you slither – maybe you're rejected, or want out, or something programmed, like alarms, that go off when you cross a threshold, open a door.... Love – the gift you can't refuse, that withers before you cram it in a vase....'

'The money thing,' says Manlio, ready to leave and angry. 'There's nothing here – so, is that a pretext or a metaphor? Money – an affair of state, like revolution? States have the mints, but money isn't only made in those, it's generated in our work, the fiddling and the expectations ... and Elodie – she doesn't deal in notes and promises, scrip and assay marks. Elise is her lighthouse – but where there's light, there's rocks. Elise feeds on images: Elodie is image, the debtor, subject of some hope, some past....

'But now, Elise wants certainty, the thing, the *Ding* that you can hold. The rock that wrecks, that you cling on to. Success, recognition, love gained, love lost and love abused. Yes, for her, it's cash. It *could* be cash. Cash loaned or earned: the only concrete thing right now for her is work that's paid and has been done.... Elodie has none of that, she's under siege, alone and cramped. The worst that's coming she must experience as her best, as destiny.... She's nothing, nothing but her fear, her trembling.... Death as The End. That fits the rules.'

'This tree of life,' I say, making the peace. 'Maybe Elodie could draw or sculpt one, quick as quick, then let's be off, honour is satisfied, the bargain's been respected, and the money, already spent, invisible....'

'Oh no,' says Elise, furious. 'No bodging! Nothing botched, and nothing forced. No rushed jobs, nothing trivial and literal for me....'

'I see for you it's logical, Elise,' says Manlio, impatient. 'If there's no tree, there should be something else – like money. Or an explanation. What it was spent on, what evil was at the root of it....

'If there's no answers, then Elise is right: it's martyrdom for Elodie. And if there's no room for the tree to grow, there is no promise, no restitution.'

It's neat, I think. But – we all stay where we were. Except – I shift my passion, undeclared and unrequited, from Elise, spoilt and short-sighted – to the tragic Elodie, who glances past me to our back-up man, the strong unscrupulous Manlio.

We like to think he follows what we say, defends us: but it's never so....

And Odette ... what tree, what life? I wonder.

Her doing good was always doing bad to someone out of sight – so now, the doing bad may be perverse as well ... someone will profit. That's what economics says.

*

'We'll come back tomorrow,' Manlio says, 'when it's decided.'

Wasted time – time's in his pockets, and he thrusts deep into them, so no more waste can get in. 'We'll go and dance, Torsten and I,' he says.

'I only dance if it gets really wild,' I say. It's out of place – it spoiled his angry mood and made me look a fool....

'All this movement,' says Elodie, 'the stupid pretexts.... The neighbours think it is a plot.... People from rich places, like you seem – it's not a good repute. I've nothing, you want it, all I've got and spent. Do you want me to go, to stay, to work for you, love you, respect you? Spin out an answer, respond to something, Elise.'

'Those – are all good options, Elodie,' says Elise. 'I want something definitive, that resolves it all, so I can think of something else. Or – live with the consequences....'

'I'm mystified,' says Manlio, as we leave Elodie, look for a place to pass the night.... 'It's not clear where it's getting us, this wandering – it's your forte, Torsten, like the bus that took us to Tenochtitlan ... you, babbling of sacrifice, how there in Mexico the good life comes right at the end, the celebration, then the death. Elsewhere, the death comes first, and then the sacrifice reverses it.... The good life is suspended till you decide what it might be....'

'You have to follow, Manlio,' I say. 'Follow the thread, do exactly what I say, pick up my references. The world is a circular round strip, you spin it if you have strong wrists, the after is before, is imminent, it's gone, and so are you, before you know what shape you have, how high you jump, how low you creep....'

'Your rambling, Torsten, isn't educative,' says Manlio. 'No lesson, and no movement, no story that we recognise and follow – no getting better or got worse. Just on and on until you can't.'

He's right. I'm twin to Elise, to her mind and destiny. It isn't what I want. She invents tests for everybody else, to see how high, how low ... and when they disappoint, she's satisfied. And if they can surpass themselves – she's miffed.

'I hadn't thought,' Elise had said. 'How desperate, how tragic, how courageous Elodie must be.... It's not attractive, though. You can't feel affectionate for her.'

'One day,' says Manlio. 'I give Elise. To sort it out. Then I take Torsten, and we leave. Us two.'

We should have helped Elodie – I don't know why, each of us had decided to take what we could and leave her – as she is. Or as what will become of her.

*

I and Manlio, we take a room – over the balera. The dancing's wild until the dawn and we don't sleep. Elise – has gone, somewhere. Restless. It's good – Manlio and I can't stand her.

The morning's stale. Fish canneries, sheds both sides of grey, narrow streets.

*

Up the hill, to Elodie's. No humans, lots of dogs and someone's put the rubbish out, it's mostly melon rinds.

There's no one in the house. 'Why did you come, Manlio?' I ask. 'There's nothing here, the whole country is a husk, gnawed by every kind of pig.'

'I was promised half of what Elise got,' he says.

'How could you be so stupid, Manlio,' I ask. 'Elise – she doesn't keep a bargain, and her word is tin.'

'I'm stupid, like you say, Tosten,' he says. 'And you? Bed? With one or other? For a little cash, you can have a different bed each night, sleep sound, and in the morning it's a different city, different language, different sights. And you feel good.'

'I'm a romantic, Manlio,' I say. 'I seek the tree of life, just like Elise.'

Manlio – he'll make his trip worthwhile some other way.

It comes to me: he'll sell her, Elodie.

He's the expert in being bad, that's clear.

He'll do what Elodie most fears: betray.

Like what her lover, Elise, already does.

*

We wait around all day, take turns to leave the hill, and have a drink. We're both quite pissed by evening. At the airport, there's Elise. 'It didn't work out, nothing does,' she says, and cries, to stop us asking more. By then I'd go to jail for Elodie.

She hasn't come; it's all a torment, being here, and leaving here.

When we arrive back at the start, Manlio salutes us, says, 'I did all right, eventually. I'll leave you here....'

There's a red 'M', and down the steps beneath he goes, he disappears.

There was a movie once called 'M'.

'Tell me, Elise,' I say. 'There is, there was, no money, but it stands between us. Tell me everything....'

'You're greedy, but you don't digest,' she says. 'What you're told lies, ferments, in a secret stomach, bubbles, ready for regurgitation....'

'And Elodie?' I ask. 'Sold and betrayed? No money and no cause.... Running, caught...?'

'She is a saint,' Elise says. 'I can't share a scene with saints. I gave some money to the group, Odette and I. They are no more. Fugitives, guerrillas, conscience of the people.... Armed struggle. No one knows where, except – we all know where. They're dead, dispersed.

'Maybe I didn't think what they might do with all that cash. Arms? Bribes? New lives? Books, for goodness sake!'

'Oh, I'd be for them, the saints: their politics is up to them,' I interrupt, and Elise says,

'The money always disappears – it's not to do with politics: it's ransoms, blackmail, preparing safe places that aren't that at all. Elodie – she could have come with us, but she preferred....'

To be betrayed.

*

'If you were lovers, now you aren't, of course she wouldn't come with you,' I say.

‘At least that seems the truth,’ she says. ‘She wanted martyrdom, rather than me....’

‘You didn’t want her anyway. And it’s not martyrdom, if you’re a warrior and fall – that’s what they do, that’s what they’re for,’ I say.

‘The story’s that,’ Elise says. ‘There’ll be no more. I’ve changed, written myself out. I don’t exist for her. And if she was betrayed and sold – there’s nothing more to do. They seek them out in rhythmic swoops – the cops; know everything. Then there’s the irregulars, and comrades who resent, shutting mouths, some cutting throats.... It’s serious, like being lovers isn’t, and taking snaps is not.’

‘I think we made things worse, Elise,’ I say.

‘That’s an opinion,’ Elise says. ‘Best keep it to yourself.’

*

It’s a grown-up world, Elodie’s, that makes you feel a kid. Your life is play-dough, theirs is laughter, too, but you’ve no right to judge, join in....

‘Don’t build them up,’ Elise says. ‘They don’t have time for you.’

‘I think they’re right in that,’ I say. ‘What they want to make of me – I don’t measure up. I’m stuck, I’m bones that reached a limit. They won’t stretch.’

‘What do we tell Odette?’ she asks.

I like that – a conspiracy. That, I understand.

I start to dream of Elodie. She starts to talk to me, concerned, some strategy, some lines uncrossable I don’t understand. Before I answer, I’m awake.

*

'Comrades? A cause? Justice and spies, the future ... you've seen my work, Torsten, heard me deride all that,' Elise says, hectoring. 'You know – it's not me, even if I say "yes" to some of that, I don't *do* "yes" to any of it. I don't need to, and if I'm threatened, then I understand not to respond. I don't know what I'd do. A band, secret society, an army? ... Suppose I'm an accomplice? Or that I don't agree with them ... what happens then? A vote – an excommunication?'

'You won't need decide – some guy in headquarters does that for you,' I say.

'Exactly so,' she says. 'It shows I don't know beans.... But I do see consequences – they don't depend on you, they come anyway. It's what will happen, that you ought to know it would. It's a cloud. Snaps don't take those well.'

'All the arts find difficulty presenting the future, Elise,' I say. It doesn't soothe.

'We could have children, Torsten,' she says. 'I don't like them. I don't like men's saliva that they think is sexy. I always think of those Kimono dragons – they slobber too. No kids, not permanently, but sometimes when you think of death, their little shrill voices and nonsense talk makes you go all over tearful....'

'Growth, maturing, everything replaced ... them taking over, you not being anywhere,' I say. 'The slipperiness of your existence – now it grows, then wanes ... the wheels are oiled with grave-juice, dear Elise....'

'Yes,' she says, 'that's it. I don't feel it often or for long, but it's true. You know how to say it, and that's easier than making art. Suppose Elodie was my child, not growing up. Always the same, fixed, to be protected, loved. Incapable of giving love – just lovable by nature. I must protect her with my body, with my life. Or she's my mother – not loving me. And – I'm the child who deserts.'

She cries. For different things, all at once. It's a torture, and it doesn't stop.

*

'It's over,' Odette says: 'It's the law. Tree life. Nothing you can do. It's a cycle, like politics. That idea we had didn't work at all. Think of Elodie as a jewel, a nugget, underground. One day we'll find her. In the end, though – it wasn't about cash, but about love and duty. Not at all what I'd in mind. Here's something else....'

ODETTE'S QUEST FOR POWER

'People read messages,' says Elise. 'Especially if they're stuck on someone else's mailbox or front door. Even obscene ones on a wall. And morals – stories that have an end, a curly tail, like bacon pigs – you can poo-pooh the convention, the naiveté – but a well-turned plot, like well-turned legs – it keeps your mind off what really matters to the people that we know: work and sex. And holidays.

'Most people – we don't see them: they don't count. They don't have holidays.

'What Odette wants – and we're her acolytes – it's difficult. What is it for, her power? What's it about? I think I live in life: but, mostly, stories, pictures, aren't. They tip their hats to what is real – they aren't. My pics....'

'Lie in a file, or in the garbage – unseen,' Odette says, bustling in. 'Like your woman, Torsten, your Sakine. She was the picture you had made of her – you tore it up, and yet you grieve. That's weak and stupid, Torsten, dear. The point is – do something real. Then, if you want, embroider it, make it an epic, game of figurines.'

'I want to do what I like, as I like,' says Elise. 'Even if it's no good and doesn't satisfy.'

'I want a rock, to feel safe holding on, then I can shout,' I say. 'Help!'

Odette's appalled. 'No rocks left, Torsten,' she says. 'All occupied. And uncertain artists – they fill the earth, Elise.

'Find me a tulip equivalent – the tulip mania boomed and busted – I'll know when to quit, rise on the boom and use the fortune to make another one, immense ... something that rides on something's back – making nothing, but diffusing. Deliveries, programmes, service of services, tax-farming, bail-providing, outlaws ransomed, contractors contracted.... That's the now!'

It's not enthralling. 'No,' I say. 'Not for me, Odette.'

ALMOST ALONE AT LAST

'You're on the run,' Felipe says, 'so you must sleep. It's difficult, here in the dorm....'

'How do we start, Felipe?' I ask. 'I'm used to being robbed: how do we get some pay?'

'Some distinctions are quite delicate,' he says. '"My friend's a thief, he mustn't steal from me." "I paid my debt, but I still owe, it's more and more." "I had to punish my best pal – I hate the guy who made me." ... Sound innocent. Maybe it's only fine distinctions that don't operate for us. Those, though, are complex situations.'

He moves away, he doesn't need a partner.

'Help me, Felipe!' I plead. He's eaten through; brown and stringy, a branch that beavers gnaw to make a dam. I cling to him.

'Well,' he starts. 'There's circuses. Put up the tent, then you can go and rob in village houses. You've the tools....'

'The animals....' I start.

'They're us,' he says. 'We're them. Exotic ones. Once we did tricks, were trained – they're pasteboard now, but snap them, and they look real real. Time's effaced that way....'

FELIPE

She gives me flashbacks, flashforwards – evocations of markets, dumps. The flowers shredded with no sale, birds vandalised. It's true; those are free and cost you everything.

'It's like old times,' she said. 'They were unspeakable. Keep quiet. Watch out.'

'Is there more to know?' I ask Felipe.

'There's fiddles every day,' he says. 'But they don't make an orchestra. Trust, believe, in nothing. Close your ears. Once you realise there's no good side, you know it all. The rest's your instinct.'

We see some jugglers, but there's no contortionists; they offended the decorum.

'Where are the circus people?' I ask Felipe. 'The strongmen, bearded ladies, dwarves, human giraffes, twins joined at the head, the Sitting Bulls....'

'They'll be around,' he says, uninterested. 'The geese!' I say, remembering. 'Trained geese! A whole flock....'

Doing goose steps, avoiding goose bumps – a delight. Until you introspected...?

There's no cruelty, no deformation now – it's good, it is miraculous. All are accepted, no one's peered at, nothing disgusts, all's nature, nothing's put on show and made to roar. I ditch the memory of the geese, poor dears, roasted in lean times ... and there were sheep! And eager dogs; and cats that climbed up rungs...!

'Elise should have been here – they crowded to be snapped,' I say. 'The flocks, the monsters, sweet, compassionate.... Gone, gone, good riddance – why, Felipe?'

'Don't let them take your pic,' he says, 'You don't know where it ends. When the tent is up, we take the pig's foot into town, and see what's loose.... What we can pick up, a door unhinged ... take only tiny much-loved little things, that leave a wound....'

'Why do we change, Felipe?' I ask. 'Is it evolution? Do we get bored? And what might we evolve towards? Fear of extinction? Does species-being grow again, like when we Sapiens lived in caves and sparred with the Neanderthals? And then, those sacred cats – once, they had splendour, now they're murdered by the whitecoats in a cage.'

He looks at me blankly, then, 'You can be sure, no one will seek your judgment, and if they did, your answer wouldn't count.'

'It's a relief,' I say. 'There are so many absences. Old wrongs.... How they suffered, the condemned – the beasts made unnatural, all circling round and playing nice. Each town inherited a colosseum with a matador.... The gentle humans, living off anomaly ... showing off their blebs.... Where, oh where? ...

'Now there's no zoos, but the whole world's a zoo. Some beasts you can pay to shoot, and others are sequestered in a paradise....'

*

The tent is up, and I remember ostriches ... they were inscrutable....

We take a crowbar, try to open village doors.

‘Remember, Torsten,’ says Felipe. ‘We’re casuals; not poor, not thieves. We don’t steal cars, we do an honest job of strength, we’re connoisseurs of awkwardness and strain. It’s true, we’re not invited in to neighbours: but we are not the foxes, the indiscriminate, the robbers. Today, we sample, apprise, leave.... It’s always, for us, day one, just like they say....’

‘It’s a thing we do, we riggers, we *giostrai*. I understand.’ I say, not quite convinced. ‘Assembling the dodgem track, the Spinner – it requires a skill.... So does stealing necklaces....’

‘As casuals,’ Felipe says, ‘we seize the mane of fortune, cling as if we’re glued, it runs and rages on with us – into the abyss, and up the Eiger.

‘“Hold on!” That is the word, the call to steadfastness: to hold our place, and not slide down, on to the street, rough sleeping.... That, Torsten, is the curse. You’re not fit for anything then....’

‘I held opinions, Felipe,’ I say. ‘Once. Women were once within my sphere....’

‘Forget all that,’ says Felipe: ‘For us, the women are a limited resource. There’s little coddling to come for us. We are alone. Opinions? Someone has thrust us down, taken our cash, our friends – the world’s like that, a pit of slime, with millions struggling to stay up high, to grasp the rim, to see the sun, the clouds, and fight the forces driving down.

'Politics – a dirty beast, Torsten: that's all you need to know. People too. You see their boots, you fear the trampling.... Catch their legs, Torsten, and down they'll go....'

*

There's heavy work, and dirty work. I start to think of letting go, of falling, landing on the street. We're casuals – I think of life, of being casual in it, being a casualty. We're not like those messengers on bikes, grinding wheels of commerce with no hands. Just doing jobs, by the day, it's habit, no one needs us casuals permanent. Work overall's like that. Irrelevant, it ebbs, it disappears. High pay or low, it's ephemeral, and so are the pale crowds that sort themselves into positions high or low.

We're different. We are the smiths, the founders – and we strike, we forge, from old iron comes new steel....

*

'This is a little place,' Felipe says. 'The circuses and fairs come round, like death and tumblers on a medieval clock. Like seasons, months. You're right – there's countries where there's millions, like us, doing all the work – casuals who fight each other every day to live to fight next day. In India – there's millions, flies sucking up spilt dal.

'We're fortunate, Torsten,' he goes on. 'Here, we're few. There's not much we can do, and we're the only ones who do it.'

And on he talks. We're fortunate!

It breaks our backs.

'We're free, Torsten,' Felipe says. 'The freest persons in the world. Our labour's sold direct, by us.... We are the contrary of slaves.'

It's not quite so: there are the corporals who hire, our middlemen. There's no philosophy in what we do. It is necessity. It's good. It isn't good for me. It's hefting stuff: disposing of detritus – not the soft job, delivering, with licences, gadgets that break, everybody waiting round, complaining.

We take orders, but we execute at once. There's secret things, of course. We're hands, and arms and legs. We have no voice, no eye to wink. Set big rockets in the vertical. Dig graves and fill them in. Take off the tags from soldiers, leaving the green.... Conceal the moribund, put them in sheds: place traps, and open cages for the animals bundled from their refuges.... There's cleaning: homicide and suicide, all the mess ... there's the bombings, gas – 'We are the flies and vultures,' I say. 'We make the landscape, polished and bare.... We know the consequences of all there is.... Responsible for nothing and for everything. It's revelation, Felipe. We see the end, but by our lifting, burying – we make it so the end is never finished, never ends....'

Felipe takes it up, he bellows, 'Casual's the style, and casual's the pay! Mounds raised, holes dug – war crimes a speciality, hidden and exposed. Epidemics managed, spills wiped and shootings covered up ... mountains moved, tombs emptied and gold dug, rare earths discovered, beans planted, cotton harvested, jeans dyed, friendships cemented over, rivers dammed, and people damned and gone for ever, objectives concretised and tarmacs maximised, palaces demolished before they're built ... all their occupants blown to dust....' And on he sings – a rhapsody. 'Loyal sons of all regimes, construct, destruct – always the same cycle – and it takes us casuals, who know it all and never tell a tale, to give it shape: or make it disappear.'

'It's so,' I say. 'We make history, with our shovelling. The epic is in landfill, where we dump the nobles and the royals....'

*

When you know these things – you know it all. It's time to rest, return to where there's still illusions: that there's constancy, and permanence.

Dear Felipe – the world will need rely on him alone.

I'm off.

He says, 'And I can do it all, Torsten. Down with the old, on, up, with the new –'

He waves his spade as I depart – Felipe, ideal for holes, ideal for heaps, for dykes and deeps....

THOR. . . .

'Thor!' Odette shouts. 'Torsten! What an adventure! Using your hammer to pay for your bed! Staying clean, staying pacific. Not being caught, not for anything, done or undone....'

'It's not a revelation, Odette,' I say. 'Labour. It's tiring, on and on it goes. It ploughs deep. Real life – It's different: a lantern slide, lit by a guttering candle. The ghastlies and the ghostlies prancing round.'

She calls Elise, and says to me:

'Life, Torsten? This? Yes, it could be. You left me – now, you can see, I am your life – live me!'

I don't believe a word.

*

Elise says, 'I've got a show! Your world, Torsten, see, it supports mine, but mine is high, sees clear the clouds, the squared-off fields....'

'Your world, Elise, could well be underpinning mine,' I say. 'Your consent, complicity – values and interest. They underlie the rest. You thinkers, you creators – need us to plant the fence, erect the trees.

'The galleries you pay? You are another sparrow: flies in, gets some reviews – and off you go. We casuals – we have no face, no name. Our enemies and allies – go up and down and round like chargers on the roundabout. But we – we're always needed, always there – anonymous. There's a lesson, there always is, though I can't see exactly what.'

*

Felipe – certainly, he had a name, but now his face is just another Southern mask – too dark for the Maghreb, too light for Mali – a face from the Sahel, from in between, Africa and Europe? Just like mine. Just a face, a piece of skin stretched over boney white.

*

'My pictures, Torsten – they're wonderful,' Elise says. She's right. They are – of clouds and sea. Quite out of fashion, ludicrous, indeed; though in New York she'll sell them all. Then make some more, and then –

'I'm sure I'll need you Torsten,' Odette says. 'My puzzle is – how to carve a realm from this increasing devastation. Loyalty I need, not from the cowed and insecure. I need to be the warrior boss, dancing with his crew, the blackguards, lovable pirates, cherished by their audience, rascals every one, but make you full of pride....'

'All *ersatz*, but it gives a boost,' I say. 'If you've not tasted the real thing ....'

'I *am* the real thing, Torsten,' Odette says. 'It's you that ducks and gutters in the wind.'

'Life can be troublesome and tedious,' I say. 'The details. Getting on with people. Love, not love, loveless – all that; which fascinates. People love to hear about it – kids, work and money: how the others manage or do not. It repeats, identical, over all places, every people. It's our obsession. Odette is right: it matters more where the materials come from, how you make a glaze, a yellow colour, or a rose.

'Where's the caravan, stuck in a sandstorm? You must know....

'We each have talents – I move around, talk differently to different people. I'm not employable for long. You have money, Odette, and want more, and to use it, show you're strong. That's it. That's all you want. Fascinating....

'Elise betrays everyone so she can be alone, squint through a lens – she doesn't trust her eyes, her vision. There has to be a machine, spies it all out for her, then she brews up stewpots of bromides in the dark. Cooks up a picture.

'Each for their own, Odette.'

THE TREASURE

'You're a marvel, Torsten,' Odette says. 'You can do anything. I can throw you off my cart – but you're an animal that always lands upright. You know, owning money in these days – it's like a plague. The people spit on me when I pass by – it's not for luck, I promise you....'

'The more you see, the more there's to forget,' I say. 'Money – no one forgets that. For us, the poor are forever on another page. The real poor, not just like us, being without. For us, it can change....'

'That's the spirit,' says Odette, cheerfully. 'I believe being a benefactor will bring me profit. The donation of a treasure – lends you lustre, especially when you've lost your cash.'

'There's lots of pictures, other stuff – even the Amber Room,' I say. 'Lost and found. Abundance restored: a pillaging, in other terms.

'One more daub tracked down, dug up, is tedium. A crust, cleaned of its overlay of crusts ... another virgin steps out, unspotted, pure and dull. And if it's painted by the butcher's little boy, some experts bribed to show its authenticity – good for the boy. So what, for everybody else.'

'Don't second guess me, Torsten,' she says. 'My gift is special. And, I'm throwing Elise out – she's a success, and even more a bore.... Now it's your turn. Win my heart, or lose your name. Don't trust to luck, not ever. Fortune passes over us like clouds ... they portend rain, but sometimes – they forget.'

‘I’m your agent, Odette,’ I say. ‘That means I do the things you won’t. I hope you don’t yearn for prolonged deaths, and stick that on to me ... What do you want? Tulips? Or unicorns?’

‘Nearly that, Torsten,’ she says. ‘Being altruistic is supposed to be a good. I want you to tramp the road again, and bring back – what brings you happiness. Or leave it where it is – but: happiness! If you are happy, for sure, it will work for others too. I’ll gift it to a gallery, a museum.’

‘Happiness?’ I ask. ‘It’s a good trick. Fulfilment? Ecstasy? Not with a person – it would be tough on them....

‘It seems a throwback: Ixtlan? The blue bird? ... Dialectics of liberation? America, the pursuit of world domination....’

‘Don’t complicate,’ she says. ‘We all know what a happiness is. Play it as it should be played, the tune is ancient ... everyone will hum.’

‘The good part,’ I say. ‘Is – it’s not a picture. Not a box, and not a scene, and not Elise. Not you. It will be my choice. I’ll have to go everywhere, and that will cost you lots.’

*

‘It’s a copout,’ says Elise. ‘Why should you seek happiness?’

‘It’s a job, Elise,’ I say. ‘A fancy. See how fragile everything is – a general strike, a catastrophe enforced – it all falls down. No “new economics”, no “make only what you use”. It’s not enough. We outran ourselves, our desires, inventions, and what there is: materials. We should have stuck to camels: died at thirty. Now we’ll pay. Happiness? – it’s all that’s left. What did we learn from flying over in balloons? From revolution? The Americans wanted to rule the world, quite democratically, they said – and see the nonsense! Every rascal was an ally, no one asked anybody what was good for them....

'Happiness – could be subversive, and it's all that isn't monetised and busted. It's all that's left – the faun's afternoon. The decadence. How right! How right for you, Elise, what you evoked.'

'My work is all emotions, Torsten, every one; not just creating an illusion,' Elise says. 'Not play. Emotion is the source, but not the object.'

'And for that you want a recognition? Is that your happiness? Is that beneath it all – nothing to do with pics and snaps, Elise,' I say. 'Your truth – just self-regard and foppery? And you, putrefying in Odette's pay, having betrayed poor Elodie – my comrade, though I didn't know her....'

'Your unacknowledged comrade, Torsten,' says Elise. 'And you know the saying – don't bet on losing hands. You didn't yield.... Well done! Well lost!'

'Odette has sent me off,' I say. 'It's a challenge, but I'm free. Her cash is perilous, it disappears, and on the way, corrupts....'

'You should have stayed with me, Torsten,' says Elise, satisfied that I will not. 'Forget Odette, as she will you. Once, you could travel round in peace, but people now aren't curious. They've crossed from curiosity to being paranoid.

'War and poverty – we're back again to where we were, before we were deluded that we could conjure riches up from air and speed.

'You didn't watch my photos – there's no people. It's not a devastation: it is absence. The beauty left to be picked out when eyes have gone. The show is called "blind landscapes" – the world when no one's there to see; no shaping eye, that gives perspective, balance, and proportion. All that, we humans added: I see that now, when it has gone.'

'It's terrible, Elise,' I say, bewildered.

'That's so,' she says. 'It's what there is when we are not. *If* we are not. Reflect, Torsten: – can you voyage in a no man's land? Without a caravanserai, without the Sufi ostlers spurring you to faith, and tying up your animals? Not giving tenderness, for sure, but certainty and diligence....'

*

I think this over. Elise says, 'Maybe you didn't understand. Happiness – is all there is that lasts, all the rest's ephemeral, if it's not already gone. Odette finances you – that's all. The only emotions ever are your own.'

'I'll betray her,' I say. 'Though – already I feel bad. I'm not the treacherous type. I suffer....'

'No one ever sees how it turns out. Everyone feels bad. Nothing lasts. That's good, that's bad. Take it any way,' she says.

'It isn't so,' I say. 'I'll show you.'

'There is bad?' she asks. 'Unequivocal? And on and on it lasts that way? I'll grant you. Amid the cruelty of everyday life – yes, I can believe – in addition to the happenstance, there could be determined practitioners of what is wrong....'

'We all know that, Elise,' I say. 'We reproduce, we do not love.'

'How will you manage, sallying out, without a net to catch you in?' she asks. 'Without surveillance, no cameras alert? No one will see you, Torsten! How can you confront that? Not to be seen....'

THE SEARCH – WITH GUSTO. . . .

You go to the beginning. It's an Alice question, finding the right rabbit-hole. Be very very careful. Even about rabbits.

This green-brown stream – should be a huge river, its energy lighting the streets of Leipzig and Yangzhou. It doesn't move.

There's a small crowd of people, big-bellied, unclothed, on the bank. I go up close, not too close –

There's splashing – a jaguar is battling a croc. He's winning. I thought of jaguars as lithe ... creatures of pointillisme, their tails paintbrushes for touching the forest with vermillion and ochre ... a splash. Expressionism at its purest.

Not at all.

He's small, robust – he doesn't feel my tabu at fighting with the reptiles. He's right in, jaws closing behind his victim's ear, the croc with her jaws open, frozen in spasm. Slowly she dies, and the jaguar drags the grey-green cadaver, the spent submarine – up the steep bank, disappears with her, and leaves us hearing him, his growling and gobbling, tearing, sucking....

'It isn't a croc,' says the guy stood beside, 'but a cayman. They're scarce. It eats fish that get poisoned by Mercury.'

I recall our balloon, with Mercury up there; inoffensive, domestic, spirit of laptops....

'Gold,' says Murilo, the guy. 'Arsenic. And human shit.... It all pollutes.'

'I struggled to find you, Murilo,' I say. 'You're on a map, but not how to see you. This battle: it started this way, it's how it will end. Survival; survival betrayed by happenstance. There's no side to be on, though, we favour furry types.

'Caymans, snakes and worms – remind us of death, its sting ... being pulled under the waves, to somewhere we are alien, out of our element ... our primal fear, like Jonas: being swallowed whole and kicking, staying down there undead, alert.

'Being digested, melting in gut acid, features eroded ... you're turning, smoothing out, into an oblong; full of feeling and brain: a sentient gobstopper, slipped down, untasted.

'The cayman's been static for a million years, taking its buffet from these river-banks. Once in its tracts, its fluid – you can see signs, "this way to the anus", "tickle the throat: hope for a vomit" – a last belly laugh from your brothers and sisters, careless or somnolent, fallen or dropped, thrown in the flow, consumed as flotsam. Their last twitch, gripe, a nauseous joke.

'No hope! – you're supine, dissolving, a chocolate bar ... Mars unarmed ... just time for a swift reliving *in nuce* of your life and of your hopes, deferred and then abandoned.

'Being torn apart is more familial, more a festive play ... we've all known that in metaphor: seen it for real in arenas, at bay with the lions ... mauled, eaten in snippets. Captives, apostates and killers – that's who we are, how we end. Civil war, Murilo. That is our destiny....'

I talk on. He's stopped listening.

The jaguar's banquet's at its end. There's leftovers – they are copious.

'I know why you come here,' he says. 'We're your fathers, unageing, surviving – just. We're your ancestors: threatened and yielding, living for real the primal scenes you think you recognise from literature. A romance, an inspiration, a beautiful idea. That's us.'

'I'm different,' I say. 'I know I talk too much, emote. It's useless. I leap from fruitless bough to bough, but all the same – I travel, think....'

He nods, has heard all this – one of the feathers on his head pinks my eye.

'I live: you feel,' says Murilo. 'I'm eaten: and you rot.'

'Then for you, there's no secret, nothing to take away,' I say. 'You know it all. If someone isn't here in their totality – they're something, somewhere else. There's no mode of your thought here that we can parse and synthesise, or take away, enjoy, take it as ours....'

'No,' says Murilo, 'that's right. You've understood. You can visit us and take away some understanding, and that's it. You can't take away our life and what we feel, and make it yours. Or if you do – you've destroyed us, your treasure. Our treasure. It can't be monetised or traded, trafficked, copyrighted. My life is unrealisable in any terms but being here, and being me. You cannot live a scrap of me – my colour or my song, my spirits, wars, medicaments....'

'If I were you....' I start to say. He waves to me: be quiet, reflect.

'Just for one day a week....' I go on. 'It's useless. You can't go here – it's not "back there" for me. You're stuck with what you are, and if you think you've got from someone else their happiness – it isn't what they had. What you take is different from what there was, from what they had.

'You, me, watching the fight, the splashing and the rest. We've seen quite different scenes.'

It's so, and so banal. There goes Odette's mission. Can't be done.

I should refund the cash advance. But – Wait!

HAPPINESS REVISITED

People go to forests, seeking the secret. Were we meant to be, or were we once, a happy species? Is this the beginning we should seek? Or is it the end, and we a part of it – bringers of death, extinction? Happiness – it's ephemeral, of course – but does it – can it – truly exist? Is Odette's mission quite impossible?

*

'Yes, it is. Of course,' Murilo says, 'but suppose it was the contrary? Suppose the sages had a point – like travel agencies have said: go somewhere else, find love or happiness, or anything at all.... And screw the people you might get it from – they're in their history, like you are, confined. Think of *Capital*. It's not an easy read, not user friendly: – but now we know, the values attributed to socialism – what's taken as real cream, straight from the cow, *Echt Schlag* – they're all quite false! and when discussed – they're not in that book, and reason, freedom, don't bring happiness.

'Socialism's desirable because it's economics. The tome, and all its siblings, are about the allocation of what can be produced, and how. That's all. Accumulation, primitive and avid, its crude and suicidal ways will pass away. We act according to necessity, not in hope of a fulfilment.

'Comes socialism: it will happen, we survive. The species will be as miserable as before.... Or, if it doesn't happen – we all die, there's no one left to say it was a shame, millions of years will pass, new worms and lizards will take power, the caymans will go on, the jaguars will find it difficult....'

'Your thesis, Murilo,' I say. 'It isn't new....'

'How could it be?' he asks. 'In Brazil, we had the best brains, then all started falling down....'

It's hot, there's little shade – I'm feverish, and where the foliage is dense, there's animals unknown and curious. Where there's just stumps, I feel exposed, misunderstood. I'm sure there's not a side I should be on.

'My idea's not difficult,' Murilo says, waving upwards to the trees.

I see his feathers, ochre and vermillion. Some rare bird. We smell the decomposing cayman, half eaten, in the undergrowth.

LIFE, LIBERTY, AND THE PURSUIT OF DRAGONFLIES

'Which do you suppose is harder,' asks Murilo, 'to produce something from nothing, or nothing from something? I shall keep the question strictly on the level of our creativity.

'Ideas, language, books, pictures – all that. Take "history": – a parallel narrative; quite different from reality – centuries of events, jumbles ... happenstance to different gatherings of humans. So, parallel to what, exactly? Not parallel to reality – reality is unparallelled.

'The story of the species – at once it's terribly slow, and terribly abbreviated. Part, is ideas produced and soon discarded – those are short, and terribly long as well. Maybe a chronicle, the history, we're not really suited for? We don't interpret our story well at all. We don't grasp what we write, what it says, and what it signifies. For someone out there in the field – history always sends out contradictory messages. They're sent to no one in particular – all random and ephemeral. Bottles tossed into the sea by thousands, castaways: different messages: no destinations whatsoever.'

'You're brilliant, Murilo,' I tell him.

I move away a little – being clothed, even quite casually, beside a fat guy almost naked, brown nipples with flat tops, a navel picked out in red with something black inside: it is unsettling. My fault, prudish, embarrassed? Well, there it is.

'Brilliant,' I tell him, 'but all sounds quite familiar. You and the sages had simultaneous revelations – a commonplace: not miracles or magic. It's only brains colliding – all made in the same way. All identical in how they work, so even metaphors communicate.... There's differences too – brains jigger, according to the time and place.....but in the end, they are machines, like animals....'

'I can't help that,' Murilo says. 'I'm stuck here, in the forest. Not an easy life. How can I check my thoughts that may not have been thought before? And isn't that the point? If we were all original, we wouldn't understand a thing that other people say and think.'

We ponder this. My gaze – it wanders.

'That's an enormous snake,' I say. 'You know the nature here, Murilo … do we stay? Or run?'

He pokes it with a toe. It isn't clear: did it move, sluggish and moribund? Is it a trunk, a branch, disguised as snake, as a snake would say?

'Let's start again,' Murilo says. 'You're a snide type, Torsten. When you say "nothing" you mean the ideas we have, that swarm and die, no corpses visible, no end, and no beginning. Nothing: the immaterial. Coming from nothing. Starting, ending as a nothing.

'It isn't that at all. The past's a nothing now, but it was once, for sure, a heap of somethings. The future – it will come, we know, we have foretold: it's nothing now; it will be something.

'You see, it isn't "hard" at all, not problematic, to have a past, a future. To have had something – and then nothing. And vice versa. It's not an inventive, literary thing, a play, a ploy.

'An idea about reality? In the forest, we have those all the time. We know it – there's reality. Lots of something. Good science, you would say. Then, there's our song and dance – we hope to coax reality a little bit our way – some rain, some sun ... some food. Is that art, religion? Or a nothing? Science it is, deployed, for sure....'

'I cannot argue with you. You have words, but they've no context,' I tell Murilo.

'Well,' he says. 'At least I'll choose our duelling weapons. What can suit? – pistols or *curari,* Torsten? Which is your choice?'

'No, Murilo, friend,' I say. 'I'm not in the battle, not at all. I don't care if you are happy. I suspect you're not. But maybe I could spot some happiness – carry it off, without you losing it, or even, if I'm rascally – gaining it entirely, leaving you with nothing: nothing at all.'

'Maybe you could,' he says. 'It's of no consequence.'

'Of course,' I say. 'I know you're not part of my world, its perceptions, its aesthetic,' and he replies, 'No, of course I'm not. But here I am, in your concrete, in your reality, as well as mine.'

'I don't see how it matters,' I start to say – then I see his trap. It's like a basket – trees are bent, and when you stray there, maybe thinking pleasant thoughts – you trip the trap, and up you go, into the canopy, startling the beasts, the monkeys and the flying things, the climbing parrots and the millipedes. We're in the concrete, both together – but I am trapped, and he is pouring it.

The answer is – I can't take happiness from his life!

'We have the same defect,' he says. 'You seem to make sense, though I don't agree with you – but – you don't know a thing. You've no analysis. Your quest for happiness – what is that? Something? Nothing?'

'I have thoughts,' I say. 'But no hard arguments. I flit from circumstance to mystery. I'm curious. Anything definitive – it escapes me.'

'It's time to hunt. It all tries to escape. And then we eat,' he says, and grins.

EAT AND BE EATEN

I don't feel hungry – on my leaf the flesh, if it is that, is greeny-grey, and there's some scales.

'That is the best there is,' Murilo says.

All night, there's movement. Nature? Humans? Or other things. When there's light, Murilo says, 'We'll go and see my pals.'

Why not? Up high, the canopy is in the clouds. It rains up there – water – not falling down, but like a lake suspended in the leaves....

*

'I must say it,' I tell Murilo. 'Your context – it's disastrous for you. I'm sorry, I know that I and mine should not exist; and all the civilisation that is threatening you, it would be better if it didn't come at all....'

'Yes, it would be best,' Murilo says. 'But you are sneaky too, and cling to your existence, pick it out in red and neon. It threatens me, goes on, too....'

'No, no,' I say. 'It's not my thing, my field is not publicity. But neon's passé – now, can't be used.'

'Well,' he says, 'that's some good news.'

*

We take the bus.

His friends – they're in the city. Three young guys, Ian, Miguel and Tom. Three bunks and a divan, bare walls. Tom's in callipers – I say, 'I've seen old sepia photos – callipers are long long gone.'

'Maybe you look for sado-maso pics – crutches and bandages, with callipers and wounds: paralysis,' Tom says, contemptuous. He doesn't trust me.

They have guns.

'Are you resisters, defenders of the weak?' I ask. 'The persecuted, insecure?'

'No,' says Ian. 'We don't use guns. We sell them.'

Murilo is satisfied: these are his friends, he takes no part.

*

There's Paloma, sleeping here sometimes, on the move, on errands, sometimes with a partner for the evening or the night – my! she's sexy. she warns me from the start – 'No sex, Torsten! If I fell in love with you, having had sex, what would it mean? Sex gone, or sex to come – all made meaningless. Nothing. An instinct, or a payment. Wait, until there's passion, love firm and indissoluble – before that, we are strangers, hungry with love but ... I'm not your passion. And mine is not for you....'

We leave it there. It's like tomorrow's feast – a cayman in the stream, grinning: at the two of us.

*

'These guys are happy,' says Murilo. 'Ask them, and they'll say.'

Ian says, 'I come from far away, but here is better.' He wears a turban, loosely wound, henna on his beard. 'No one asks where I'm from, and no one knows where it might be. I remember – "the horses relieved their fatigue by rolling on the banks of the Indus, and shook off the saffron clinging to their manes". We'd passed through everywhere, taking something from everyone, and as a gift – moving on. Like the Mongols took writing from the Uighurs as they rode on through. Or, as the books say: the opposite. The Uighurs gave the Mongols writing as they....'

'I understand,' I say. 'Murilo doesn't set much store by happiness ... he goes the long way round – there's nothing in the story of us all, or any metaphor, to say we are, have ever been – a happy crowd.'

'I'm satisfied,' says Miguel. 'We get supplies, so we can sell.... We make a bargain, not an arm.'

'Who sells the arms to you?' I ask.

'The army and the cops,' says Tom, trying to straighten up: 'We don't deal here, not in this room. Here's crap.'

They have fine suits to do the deals – silk shirts, silk drawers, and polished shoes, kept in a closet, specially.

They're high up, on a rock that seems it's made of dwellings, each clinging to the next, bright beads, like glass marbles, alleys, with multi-coloured filaments, a necklace strung on wires and pipes, painted over, wise sayings on the walls – as if the whole suburb could drop into the sea as one – the blue sea that's all there is except ourselves, us saying wise things and clinging on, each to the next, knowing we could all drop in the sea ... a bracelet made of links you can't unpick.

It's not what Odette meant at all, I guess.

*

'It's best you don't go out,' says Ian. 'Murilo won't – there's no trees here.' He laughs.

'I'm not worth anything at all to you,' I say. 'I feel I'm a prisoner, but I'm not constrained. Are you cautious, bound to be, in a trade that I don't understand?

'Murilo: his discourse is so complicated, and he runs ahead of me – forest and city in contrast ... and the sea is blue, so blue, the streets are feverish, they smell of pepper and of rinds. Everything does something I don't understand.'

I think of Elodie, far over on the other side, where the sea is grey and the clouds are whitish-grey, up the street come clouds, and stay all day. There, it's fascism all the time outside – and here ... there's guys with berets, blue as the waves, I don't know what they do, don't dare go out. They're armed.

'You won't learn anything by going out,' Murilo says. 'This room here's a little state, and I feel safe. They do their trade, ask nothing of me; they aren't curious, and nor am I. As for you – what do you want of them, three lads, one lame, one done jail time, and one, Ian, a joker. Ian's the one you need to watch – he asks questions – 'what purpose do you serve, Torsten? Why don't you work, you're lounging here, trying to make out with Paloma, although she's told you, doesn't go with foreigners, especially without cash....'

'I understand,' I say. 'You're busy here. There's whole countries that's full of guys that seek their happiness.... A sacred know, those holy snakes....'

'Yes,' Murilo says, 'but they're the ones that make the guns and sell them to the cops, the federals, train them too, they sell them on to you, you sell them back, and give them pride and medals too....'

*

'You are a cover for us, Torsten,' Miguel says. 'And Murilo stays here, takes up little room – he covers us, he's soft and warm....'

'I think,' Murilo says, 'but I don't act. And you, Torsten – don't think well, don't act at all.'

'Oh,' I say, quite displeased. 'I don't exist, I am a ghost. I love you all, you don't love me, you look right through. I confess, that I confess too much, I have my guilt, my suffering for all the sufferers, and understanding for you guys.... Elise – she was a ghost as well – she casts her shadow on the walls, her photos take her lymph and pus, frame them, glass them over....'

They don't know who she is – it's quite irrelevant. Elise, she snaps. That's all she ever wanted.

Paloma – lives and risks. One day she doesn't come – there's consternation, they don't look for her.

*

'We're clean,' says Tom. 'We don't do drugs, we don't trade kids, the neighbours love us – we defend; our business isn't done from here. Each lives just as they can, and if they go and don't come back, like Paloma has – this place is vast, much broader than the sea, carmine and ochre – those our colours, infinite the little paths and alleyways: this is the forest now. Where Murilo lived – it's gone and burnt. If you want happiness, Torsten – it's here if it is anywhere.

'I know,' I say. 'Murilo too – he won't go back, his mind has been prepared. He'll go to conferences and run a stall that sells street food....'

'You know what they say,' says Ian. 'Look into the abyss – it ends so the abyss looks into you. I love a scrutiny. Pep it up – shoot straight, both hands, and don't look back. What we do is legal, important – a check, a balance. If we sold rat poison, Torsten, would you say we're violent? You have this prejudice – that what you couldn't do must be outside the law, be wrong. It isn't so.'

'I'm sure the guns are stolen, Ian,' I say. 'And they go in groups to groups. Maybe they go back, back to the federals....'

I've no idea. What happens here? These guys are gruff, but if I want, I'm sure I can go out, do exactly what I like. I didn't understand the forest, or the language there.

Now, it's the city, and we all know those.... No one need speak at all, or look up in the canopy, or where to put their feet.... The city-forest – that too is coming to its end. Where next?

*

We have the light on all night, like a jail. It gives security. It gives exposure. No one breaks in to a lighted room and shoots you all. They wouldn't have a chance.

Tom moves about all night – can't straighten out. Ian chuckles in his sleep, and Miguel sleeps with Murilo, they lie embraced – a narrow bed. Murilo's feather crown stands on the floor beside – and one night Paloma comes back, beating softly on the door, she comes and lies with me on the divan. She isn't well, she's very hot and bruised.

'Hush,' she says, that's all. 'Hush,' and in the morning she's gone again, we never see her, not again, so far as anyone here has said. I miss her, I know she has turned from being busy to being sad, I can't imagine where she goes, has ever been. Her time forever found and lost, regretted and repeated. Full of fun, and now, reaping the retribution.

*

'I want out,' I tell Tom.

'Be careful,' he says. 'First, you pay us for hiding you. Then we'll say how you can leave.'

'Murilo – maybe he's endangered, so he hides. I'm not....' I say.

'We're traders of the middling sort,' says Tom. 'We're middlemen, we do not execute. We're a convenience. You hid here for months. You've money and a story – if I were you, I'd hide too ... then, you must pay the bill.'

'My cash is in the closet,' I tell Tom. 'I trust you. We are friends.'

'You were in the forest. You'd a purpose, being there, and Murilo is your friend. He's not happy – so if you want happiness, you must help him. Pay us,' Tom says. 'We at least – won't be happy, but we'll be satisfied. Murilo won't leave here – he's king in the forest. They're all kings and queens in the trees that's left, and they're all about to be extinct. If he goes back – he can be dethroned. Maybe kings are sacrificed? Maybe he's just a pretender. Do you understand all that? All pasts are over, but some are obliterated, incinerated too. You being here – means you're seeking happiness, like before, when you met with Murilo. He's a part of you. His happiness and yours ... are one. Stay, go, Torsten: pay us first.'

'I understand all that,' I say. 'That only I am subject to the deal. Only I'm to be the happy one.'

We laugh – it sounds ridiculous.

'We don't keep money in the closet,' says Tom. 'Ian hides our money. We trust him, we have to. It makes him happy so.'

'The forest....' I start to say, that it's become a sad precarious place since guys like me discovered it. Well, where's it gone, where is it now? Back in the imaginary...?

*

We leave it there, for now. I stay. Ian says, 'You have a good-sized tab – the rum and beers! I hope you've cash enough....'

'I'm not in danger, Ian,' I say.

'If you need hiding, it's enough,' he says. 'Danger is assumed. We don't do risk assessment. It makes no difference to your bill how keen your pursuers are, how many. Your mission? Making the forest be a place of happiness? It's quite a task....

'You could have been a trader,' he goes on, jesting. 'You'd keep it all a-shuffling on. We could find a camel for you.'

*

'Miguel,' says Tom. 'He's not come back. Some feisty clients – they are holding him, and must be paid.'

'Pay them, pay them!' says Murilo, crying. 'They can do terrible things.... And if they sell him on ... or even worse, they hand him in....'

'We'll have to pay,' says Ian. 'Or he'll come back in bits, slid underneath the door....'

'Really, it's your problem, guys,' I say. 'Leave my cash out of it. That's quite my business, and not yours.'

'Torsten,' Murilo begs me. 'You're my friend, Miguel is my friend. There's nothing else to do but pay....'

He's quite frantic – anyone would be.

What a scene, when Miguel comes back! We drink to him. Murilo puts on a shirt and pants, and looks like anybody else. Like any other king.

*

'No,' says Odette. 'That's it. Life is a bowl of cherries, but you, Torsten, you've had your bite.... Now comes the pit....

'It wasn't too bright an idea right at the start, and now I'm really short of cash. That's it! I'm dry.

'Elise is doing really well – she even has some sales. Right now – I'm putting up a Jessica – that's it! Putting up with her.

'The dance! Bodies in motion: – you have to know the script, the movements and the beats – you don't have time to think of nakedness, of letting go. All that, says Jessica, goes in the choreography. Use any music that you like....'

'I nearly reached my goal, Odette,' I say. 'I need the fare back, that is all....'

'I told you, dear,' she says. 'I'm very short right now. You'll have to improvise. Like Jessica....'

JESSICA

'*You must be terrified*,' she writes. '*How can I help? There's dancing everywhere. Done well, it is a substitute for cash, and tickets, plans and futures – or better, it is not a substitute at all, it's everything there is, and all the rest falls away from it like fluff, like the flock from willows, that blows into the river, disappears....*'

'*Not at all*,' I write. '*I love everything I've done, and everything that has been done to me. All's splendid and unique – and all I need is cash, to take me to the next appointment....*'

The lyric mode's not mine. It irritates.

What is Jessica?

If she comes here – she'll find some work. And me?

*

I feel I'm master of the past. The past's an open library. It's problematic, but much, maybe most, of what you need to know, is there.

I want much more than just the past. The future. These excursions I have made as spectral visitor – I've been there. I want more, I want to be in it, the future, long after my cadaver's been lost; to stay in it, to master it, not as great khan, but as a ghost, a name, kids know it, it's in songs. Seeing, as it goes on, how the future ends.

Dance isn't part of that.

I guess it's dangerous, of course it is, those are all dangerous things I've done – the balloon, the forest, all of that. On some parts of the road, there's bandits. They don't trouble you if you have nothing. You're evidently just a poor man.... All you have to do is travel, keep on moving on, not being helped, no sympathy. You don't need comradeship, you don't need anything. If you ask someone for a fare, it won't be given. It doesn't matter, not a bit....

Or – consider the experience, the people: Elodie, Murilo – they don't do communication. Their anxiety – transfused into them, their blood decanted off. Their daily flow is acid: it's old stuff, space junk, detritus, that hits you in the head – gives you their aphasia. Knowing but not recognising, speaking, and not manufacturing words: blundering. Words is only part of it – it's the situations you are in, theirs: pasted on your eyes. Lives blocked by shadows, armed, vindictive. They pass it on to us, a miasma. A hiatus, end of the line: a mystery. Chaos.

NOMADS

'Can you rope a horse?' the guy asks. 'Tell jokes, recite sermons? Drive a truck, stop snoring when you're pinched? Fry steaks, pin snakes: shoot to miss, shoot to hit, shovel mud as dense as squash ... the same colour, tons of it when the dam has burst: or the clouds: they too have burst?'

'I can drive a truck and shovel mud,' I say.

'I'll take a chance,' he says. 'I'll try you.' He doesn't say how long. It's of no consequence.

'Shovelling you do supremely well,' after a while he says, 'Now, broaden out. We want a sermon on – "the real is true". The guys will love it: take it smooth – take it any way. "Is reality the only truth?" – "only the real is true..." "the real, what is it...? How do I know I'm in it...?" In or out? Out for a smoke? In for the experience? "Is thought in the real? Is language?"

'It's old-style religion, that we understand....'

*

There's thirty guys stood round: with chaps and nooses: hats big enough to fry.

'What's a fiction?' I start off – and then I stop. If what I'm saying is one, a fiction, maybe I'm a fiction too, telling untruth, on purpose, or through my incompetence? If it were straightforward lies, for sure – I'd be a liar. But history, the being us – we're always in a hatch of lies, wanted or not....

That has a name – like 'pod of whales' – a hatch of lies is 'fiction'.

What, anyway, is a person, a being – living in error, incompleteness, lies told and lies received, lies that vie with ignorance for space inside our tattooed carapace...?

We're leaky vessels....

'I go to sermons, hear the lies, internalise. What is past is true, was, is, real: but to me, my understanding – it is the loam of falsity: turned into a tale meant to seem true, perhaps, but false. Meant to deceive. History – all that we know of the past, the real – all false....

'The future – can't exist, and so it can't be lies. But lies are told around, about, all that there is, will be. What does not exist, can – and can't – be false.'

I don't say – though it's true – that I can't tell lies from truth ... not even when it's people that dissemble, or are frank and honest. I can't tell lies from fiction, fiction from the truth. All that is, must be believed. It's caused me endless trouble.

*

This is my field – Elise's pics, Murilo's realm – it's frantic territory; the beasts, the creeping things – Murilo's subjects, like Elise's, ignorant, ignored, traduced, but partners still, like the Athenian women and the slaves, undeniably inside, with voices like the hizz of bumble bees ... muted, the bourdon of the ages. Indispensable, but mucked about, impregnated, whipped, listened to and heard, but not consulted: snapped by Elise. How she depends, wholly, on her subjects. Murilo abandoning his – they're nonetheless his substance.

I finish, there is applause – like fire-crackers. Many have sloped off. What have I said? There's lies you tell, then there are fictions, meant to be lies, meant to be truth. It's quite a dance. You pick it up....

*

Driving the black calves to the slaughterhouse – I cry.

'Nothing to be anxious for,' my boss, Jorge, says, embracing me, kissing my forehead. 'It's all ordained, their destiny, from birth, this was the end. If you regret it, you regret the whole of consequence. There is no other, Torsten. Cause and effect is our sheet-anchor – quit that, there's chaos, nothing follows other things: they jump, like smidgin mattercrumbs, hepped up in cloud-chambers, hopping like fleas on crack.... Precedence and hierarchy would suspend....'

'It's all the jail-time that I did,' I tell him. 'The gun merchants – they limited my freedom. Yes, freedom can't be absolute, I know: as with the real, the true, it has high walls and guards, and judges, guys who'll take a shower with you and cut you up.... But still, with Tom and Co., if I could leave their little house, go down the hill and watch the sea repeat itself.... I should have felt more free....'

I think of Elodie. Her house, tight and unsafe.

*

'Now, let's get on with it,' the sturdy crowd of gauchos shouts. 'Unbolt the tables and the chairs – let's toss them to and fro and break some heads.'

*

'Do you want things to be true, Torsten?' Jorge asks. 'You didn't make a case. People who want the truth don't want the consequences. It's best not to know for sure, even in a fiction. It's like Crete: you know it's all lies, so you plunge into it. The wine is excellent.

'You need be strong, to run with it, the truth.'

*

We raised them, killed them, ate them – or someone did. In principle, it's fine: a luxury, so even better. Does you good. Relax. It's fine.

The grasslands, the steppe, savanna – it goes arid, easily. The Sahara once was green and full of animals – it's hard to bring it back. We nomads – we're not agricultural, don't settle easily – maybe we make it worse.

'Don't think of that,' says Jorge. 'Or you won't sleep.'

'I don't sleep much anyway,' I say. 'I think of people.' Elodie, mostly – quite useless.

The bunkhouse is unquiet: jokes, spasms, personal noises, unexplained.

'You're a sweet boy, Torsten,' Jorge says. 'Those sermons are crap. Us nomads, now – they don't understand a difficult theme. They do things with their hands, but we've no materials. There's fascism, and there are know-nothings too.'

Jorge values me – wants to go on the road with me. A duo, fife and drum: guitar and bass. Voice and tape. With a repertoire – 'Life on Mars', and 'Maybeline'. It makes no sense. Then wild stuff: '*Da Lama ao Caos*', '*Banditismo por Uma Questão de Classe*' – those kids killed in the crash....

'I'm not sure, Jorge,' I say. 'I need the cash, but I don't play an instrument or sing. I'm used to horsing round out here....' He doesn't laugh.

He never touched me. Maybe I'm missing something – maybe he thinks so too.

'Farming,' says Jorge. 'It's on the way out. There's not enough to eat.'

'You have the vision, Jorge,' I tell him. 'It's our job to educate the people, but it's a hard and craggy climb.'

*

'See this, Torsten,' Jorge says. From beneath his bunk, he pulls a sack. 'Ferrara miniatures,' he says. Squares, like iced cakes – they're tiny. 'Not the originals – copies are better. The Masters knew that – hundreds of copies, industrial. Hans did the hands, Federico did the face, the landscape by some passing Landsknecht. You know the Italian lady in the Louvre that everyone wants to see?' he asks: '"The lady with the toothache". What a flop! You need the aura, *dusha*. It's not about paint and brushes – you have to see beyond.

'People are donkeys, Torsten – all swarming creatures are: – except that donkeys aren't! Geese: they're more like it!

'Value, my dear. What are you worth? As a corpse – hmmm. You have been used. As a skeleton? Better, a doc's prop, propped – in someone's waiting room. We're all skeletons in waiting.... Small change. But to me ... you have a value. No price. I love you, Torsten. I can do valuations – I'm a lead hand, after all,' and he laughs. 'The others in the bunkhouse – they value you, but as a replica, one of a set, replaceable. A spoon, a bridle.

'Things can be robbed – but the soul remains, hung for ever on the nail, or stashed in the bag beneath the bunk....'

'I know, Jorge,' I say. 'You're a collector, you understand value and creation – but we objects, we always slip away....'

I think of Elodie, Elise – they weren't even in my net. Jessica must have the muscles – she'll wriggle through the mesh, and off! She's in my future, a Sonia to Raskolnikov.

'Don't dissemble, Torsten,' Jorge says. 'We catch people. They're our trophies – and we're disappointed, nearly always. If you collect, you have to keep on doing it, revive, refresh. It's novelty we need – something new....'

Here in the grasslands, all's antique, even the massacre, even the military: lethargy. I could stay here with my friends, share the disaster with them. When I can't do my sermons, I would be the cook, and then the carpenter. And when I could do everything, I'd rise to be lead hand, and one night, like Jorge has – I'd leave. Take the best horse – and disappear.

*

I don't need the fare – I can take ship and brave the endless sucking sea, and then be paid.

It's what I do. It's what all nomads do, the casuals, the cowboys, know where everything is buried. Go to the port, use someone else's carnet, sign on, take ship. The sea, the sea....

Jorge loved me. It hasn't meant a thing.

*

Jessica is tall and weightless, like a chain encased in plastic, like you use to block your moto's wheel. You can roll her over your back and shoulders, like a wrestler does. You won't feel a thing, and she'll come down upright, wait for your next move. 'Go on,' her posture says. 'Throw me some more – I'm made for that, and I shall wait and see what exactly you want to do, and whether it works artistically, I mean. I don't break.'

She says, 'You were in places where you let them fuck you over, and just made a note of it, and tried to fit it in to some plan you didn't have and didn't understand? You're like an eland, big enough to resist, but wandering round defenceless, followed by your little thoughts.'

'It could seem like that,' I say. 'You take in situations, nothing happens, and when it does and everybody knows about it, if they're living – it all falls exactly as you knew it would. You don't need see a war to know when a people will fight and massacre their neighbours, or that they'll destroy their context, have to move on, drink water off runnels in the street and eat the garbage. You know that if it can, it will, it will happen exactly like you know it will.'

We don't mention it again. It's plain, it's plain to everyone.

*

'There's an immense amount of us, Jessica,' I say. 'We've pushed out other animals. To make room for us, our future – huge numbers would have to die. Will have to. The means is here, it's easy to do it, it's all set up, waiting. Only – I don't want it to happen, don't want to die.'

She tests my arm above the elbow: 'It's good not to bulge,' she says. 'But you've no balance, and no rhythm. You'll end up soon just sitting down for ever.'

'You're lazy, Jessica,' I say, irritated.

'If you've nothing important to do, you rest,' she says. 'It's planned for you. You must do what you're made for. It won't get you far, but it gets you as far as you can go.'

'So – Elodie is forcing it. Locked up and hunted?' I ask.

I told her everything.

'It's a contradiction,' Jessica says, decisively. 'All the people you've met have something like: they project, they alienate, they amputate. Money doesn't help: having it, not having it. And you – you've done the kind of work anybody wants to do less of; always. Not good.'

*

'Of course,' I say. 'I left out the kissing and the telling. Their absence conceals no surprise. It's all over the books that anybody writes. The adventures and the sex routines – always the same, always expected, always a disappointment.

'Crating alligators, shoot-outs, bandit cowboys ... what's done over scores of times – it doesn't need repeating. Use an imagination!'

'Yes,' says Jessica. 'No need to spell that out: what you caught, who trampled you. What's left, what you have told me – it's dull, but still more interesting than leaving in the saucy stuff. You, I, remember the boring part, although it isn't memorable.'

'Odette?' I ask.

'She's gone to keep her money company,' says Jessica. 'We're on our own, we don't need to work for her now to stay alive; don't need be loved, appreciated. It's the new life....'

'It could be disastrous,' I say. 'She sent me off to find my happiness. I didn't come near to it – I'm lucky to be back, with all the money spent, steering shipshapes steady on the sea....'

'Happy?' asks Jessica, and laughs. 'You could have sat here, read a paper, known you'd not find happiness where you had thought to go....'

'You mean the happiness was here,' I ask, foretasting her response. 'It was Odette? Especially her cash?'

'It's so for you, it's so for me,' she says. 'We're slaves by nature, you and I, poor Torsten. We need a boss, who can provide for us. It's sad.'

'It's compromised, Jessica,' I say. 'My standing as a critical critic, if what I need is sponsoring.'

'I need cash,' says Jessica. 'But I have talent. I'm not so sure you do.'

'If I have understood,' I say. 'Odette: her capital is spent, she and it are both in paradise. There's capitalism still – and more and more of us are poor.'

'It's in the book,' says Jessica. 'We did it all at school. "Too little is produced to decently and humanely satisfy the wants of the great mass."'

'Maybe we can plan together, Jessica,' I say.

'Maybe we might,' says Jessica. 'But I would need to trust and like you much much more than I do now, Torsten my dear.'

It's a serious obstacle, what she says.

*

I ask Jessica, 'What killed Odette?'

*

'She's not exactly dead,' says Jessica. 'She became something else. An "other thing". It's transmuted – into a legal labyrinth. She's in the middle. You can enter it, if you've the will and time. You won't get out.

'You remember Breton, "Un château à la place de la tête – c'est aussi un bazar de la charité". It started there. She grew deluded, that she was big and stony, a fortress – and that she was also handing out to us her substance ... to Elise, to the guerrillas.... That we were the charity bazaar. It was her slippage, from the world of capital, to the creative universe where one hands out the good things, puzzling, attractive, luxurious. Things without value and without price, but invaluable and priceless. Often unique.'

'All the robber barons had that urge, Jessica,' I say. 'Redemption, regret, desire to transform capital into art that would remain eternally, mesmerise the artists that made it, then their publics, with things incomprehensible, figures knocked off their plinths, away from ritual and sacrifice. These cult objects, torn from their context, became oddities, abstracted. A vocabulary grew up to elucidate abstraction – terms like beauty, the eternal – all that stuff. The 'destiny of humans', encapsulated, bought, gifted and displayed: embodied in a commode, an incision, a silver print, a lampshade ... in *Formen*.'

'Not at all,' says Jessica. 'That's banal. Odette ramped onward, on Breton's track. That was her launch – giving her the moment, the second of departure, when you know you are in movement, not under your self-control, but on a trip.

'Concrete poetry – she listened, chanted on, by the hour: the week. It started with the lines "*les chiens m'ont montré les crocs sur la route où dort l'avare*". You told her about your cayman – she felt the scene referred to her. An error, for sure – a cayman is a croc – those *crocs*, though, are probably not: not at all. She resented that. She made a will – recorded it. Concrete. Sounds, Torsten. The lawyers can't understand – who gets what, or nothing. It's noise. Syllables and banging, dancing on copper tables, howls and yowls. Fun. She is as she always is: rich and impenetrable.'

'Sane, inhuman – not human. Not one of us, but in control and plausible,' I say.

'Elise suffered terribly,' says Jessica. 'Because for her the starting point must always be the real. Odette was real, but had no reality. She cancelled it. She was beginning and the end. There was nowhere else. Nothing to develop, nothing to be developed from. No visual.'

A reputation of the middling sort, gone tomorrow – settling for recognition limited – hawking the ordinary. No one but her will care.

'It's not a tragedy,' I say. 'It's just an end, where we can't go. Everybody ends – Odette has ended, but she isn't dead. Could be for her there's not an end?'

'It could have been another thing,' says Jessica. 'Inventing a way to shift from sense to the beyond. It could have been a bomb, a germ, to end the world. Humans do that – pulling down the temple on our heads.'

*

Odette was strange – invention is. Some years – only red flowers. Others – a single silver bush. Blue birds – only them, the others shooed – she wouldn't spray others to conformity. Respected everyone – and made us hop and strut to her tunes and litanies. You remembered these, her oddities. But you forgot her exploration of the world, using us as scouts. Never discovered anything: the collections – she frittered them, sold them off on the stall she kept to buy in stuff; sold for no song – merely a trill.... Defeat acknowledged – with insouciance, and resignation. She talked to everyone, then invented language that made no sense at all, except ... we knew exactly what she meant. 'I didn't make you understand,' she said.

*

A language everybody was to learn to speak, and all the other languages, they lose their meanings, all there had been – is forgotten, and makes no sense.... As if we'd all caught an aphasia, and somehow our new fractured words had a significance, and nothing else outside them made any sense at all.... Except – the new language didn't refer to the world we all still lived in.... There were no conventions of meaning, or of utility....

'A pioneer,' I say, doubtfully. 'Odette has found a way to hide her capital.'

We gaze on that perspective.

'A simplicity, the basic forms, but not at all able to grow: abstraction staying squiggles. A life ending or beginning in the incomprehensible,' says Jessica.

'Comprehensible to her?' I ask.

'How can we ever tell?' asks Jessica.

*

She plays Odette's will to me.

'Lawyers always find a way to spoon out cash, so that some drips on their dry bread,' she says.

It's very loud: 'HOUN HARACON, BLADAREENAMOK COQQINZANAZING.....'

Absolutely genuine, her voice – and her meaning, but not ours. The sound of capital, perhaps. The song gold guineas sing in leather bags to send themselves to sleep – ready for a new day. New purchases, new travelling with guineas absolutely similar: – buying Senior's last hour? A person? Or something else entirely – a memory of absurdity, relax, an evening she must want to pass on, without the trimmings, without *crocs.*

*

'You're the stupidest kind of anarchist, Torsten,' Jessica says. 'When you were screwing Odette, you cheated, but you didn't rob. You don't know how people operate – no one does, but you were on expenses – you never saved a cent. Following orders – is that how you think you get to do exactly what you want?'

'It's much more subtle than it seems,' I say.

*

I tell her, 'I understand you perfectly, Jessica, and you do me. Usually at this point I say 'I love you' – like in the movies. But I'm learning not to. Maybe you'd like to try some holds with me? Or some *brisés*? Some *tours en manège*?'

'I don't do that kind of running, jumping, falling in love,' she says. 'I don't dance dictionary. The good thing about you, Torsten, is – if I drop you, you don't break.'

That is the basis of our relationship. More 'last days' than belle époque.

FINTAN

It was as if Jessica had invented him: Fintan. Supple, legs that locked and folded like a crane's, a stork's. A mind articulated, bending every way, but also snapping shut and straight. A horror. Throwing Jessica up, compliant – an umbrella furled going cloudwards – then a frill, a medusa, fluttering down.

Peeling philosophies – like they were mangoes, sucking them down. Short shrifts to everyone ... then changing register. Pontificating: on to marginal costs, monetising lives, neo-corporativism: – nothing survived his white fire – he sanitised and sterilised, heated and chilled. I feared him, his re-made hostile world: he deployed Jessica like she was a sword-stick, his sharp instrument....

Theses I had thought were mine, fresh-grown, original – he tracked them to their origins ... my half-remembered, half-misunderstood – my quotes and prompts ... the stuff that gathers in you, fluff from people more intelligent, more scrupulous ... not more useful.

'The tyranny of the real!' says Fintan. 'The only way to live outside it, in the imaginary – is to take money and ideas from the CIA. In Lanzhou – from the GRU. My parents....'

It's ridiculous.

'You look too young to have parents,' I say. He thumbs his nose at me.

Fintan runs everywhere – not to keep fit; to get away from things, the person he's been talking to. 'Those proto-Germans, they were right,' I say. 'Schopenhauer, the followers – you can hold up, slow down, what will happen anyway – reaction, the counter-revolution, revolutions that fail and last, the pseudo in its forms – reaction can succeed. You see its corpses, smell them. Distances away. But what will happen, happens anyway, now or later. No one can stop it.'

'That's genius,' he says. 'Or a tautology. I prefer to think – it's the latter, and that you're a pseudo-bum!' He laughs.

He picks up Jessica, runs outside with her, and they whirl. At that moment, I know I lose her, love her.

It passes quickly.

I'm back in my body.... I cancel him, Fintan.... 'paramnesia differs from the aesthetic attitude as memory differs from the imagination'. A sacred thought. I remember the battle in the river, fur versus scales. Watching, deferring – great mistakes. You must engage, everywhere, where you're not concerned: remembering; painting images permanent on nothing you can ever see.

*

Fintan will have a new economic model up his sleeve, something to do with large numbers. He'll have remedies for glut and dearth. He's certainly come here to look for money, take up with Jessica, though he says he's given up the dance.

False memory, false realities.... We let Elodie down, I should go back, find her. Join her. Save – her. Save myself.

Odette? – that scene is over.

Everyone, in a life – is mostly alone. It's good, and if not good, it's so. Everyone has something they can hold to – a rock, a fin, learning to swim: remembering how to splash back when you are going down.

Odette – we hear her voice. A performance. Orders you can't obey.

Elise – it's eyes.

Jessica – muscles. That's precarious.

Elodie – she knows the crimes, she's the avenger: they will be punished. Generations called to account, generations saved. Hers, the baldrick, the long sword of justice, hard to manipulate.

Fintan – has what he knows. Nothing.

Everyone is full of knowledge: worth absolutely nothing.

I've more than him – I'm what I've done. Memory – it counts for something, surely?

Fintan has answers, but they fit what's just been blown away—

'Destruction of the working class. Destruction of reality by means of ideas. Destruction of ideas by means of reality.' Fintan – the new certainty, new reaction. How to survive death by means of a well-managed body.

'Fintan's tremendously stimulating,' says Jessica. 'But he's a bore.'

'Yes,' I say.

*

'I have other calls to make,' says Fintan, skittering like a marsh-flame, looking through our food supply. 'But my eye's on you....' And off he goes. Too bad – that when they don't look back it means they will return.

*

'Fintan knows a lot,' I say. 'His parents – had the confidence, the ear at least, of despots, and trapped them, made a net....'

Post-imperial investments: the rulers were bound and throttled. That's how he knows it all – from archaeology to how you bind a vassal. You put the big shots at risk, but you risk more yourself.

It's better to know nothing, than to know what can get you persecuted, put in jail, discredited.

'That family,' says Jessica, 'are deep in politics, advising half the world. It gets you much resented. Next time he drops in, he'll be a different type ... much chastened.

'Details, Jessica,' I say.

'Oh, the family are in everything. Fintan's an all-round everybody. He sees his siblings, they instruct the clueless, the dummies who've wrastled to the top ... those who don't depend on his relations are tools or ornaments. So, whatever you do for him, you're never up to it, to being top: you're never good enough to satisfy....'

'Well, Jessica,' I say. 'I don't do things for people. I'm not at all impressed by Fintan and his clan.'

'To be counsellors to Princes,' Jessica says, 'you really have to want. Fintan finds it boring. He can't be a Prince, so he doesn't want to be a counsellor. His family: – they start by convincing people who are ignorant except they know they want great power: coercion. After a while, you need it to keep your head in place. Fintan's crew persuade and wriggle in by being expert – in anything: health, animals, folklore, trade, arms – anything. Then once they've found a chink, they begin taking over all the rest. You rise. You know you end by falling. Why do it? Lots do: they take the risk, although there is no risk – there's certainty. You see them at it – there's no more explanation.'

'It explains everything there is, all I have seen,' I say. 'It's reason. We all use it, even if we'd rather not; it makes us all the same, predictable. It starts by seeming an instrument that makes inventions, but soon it's quite mechanical. In that sense, we are robots; no point in making robots just to be like us!'

'You knew it all, right at the start,' says Jessica. 'Your travels, exploration; all was clear before you set off. You're not an innocent. Your path – it was a highway. You don't fool me – I don't fall. Not for anything.'

'I believe you, Jessica,' I say. 'And belief's the next step to trust.'

'Flesh,' she says. 'All flesh, Torsten.'

*

'I know exactly what I don't know, and don't want or need to know,' says Fintan. 'I thought it would come from Indonesia – but I was wrong. Too soft. It will be from Central Asia, no one expects it, there's not enough people.'

'What, Fintan?' I ask. 'What will come?'

'What no one is expecting,' he says. 'Not that it matters if I'm wrong. That's what I calculated. That it shouldn't matter if I'm wrong, and that when it ends, it should end quickly. Just for me, of course.'

'It's pretty here,' says Jessica. 'The best you could imagine. This big run-down house, the weedy garden, the patchy grass. But there's nothing left for us. It couldn't be improved on, and now it's winding down.'

*

They say here's the centre of the world.

'If anything is beautiful,' says Fintan. 'You have to find this beautiful. It is your future.'

It's grey on grey – grey scrub, grey sand, flat. It goes on and on, then there's the sky. That too ... on and on.

There's grey water in a hollow. 'That was a famous lake,' he says. 'It makes you cry. Not me – I am accustomed. The people who lived from it, and all the flocks: they cried. The level of the water stayed the same.'

A big Soviet truck takes men and women from somewhere, men and women wearing rubber boots, loads them in, bounces them off. Going to do something in the grey. If they sing, it's not audible from here.

'It's how you learn to see it,' Fintan says. 'It is stark. Over there, beyond your powers of sight, there's workings of a silver mine. We could go down and see....'

'This could be enough,' says Jessica. 'Right where we are standing now. Even too much, too strong.'

It's true. It's like an empty stage.

'Remember,' Fintan says. 'This was once a fertile place.. Horses, camels, onagers ... and traders – Indians weighing the coin and marking it. The caravans, the songs. This has been worked to clinker, it's worn out, worn through. It can be beautiful, but for the life, made of exchange, discussion – it's now useless. You might put something else in here. Move people out, bring others in – a road, a railroad....'

'Trans-Europe Express,' says Jessica. 'There was an idea to put the terminus here. Then they found it was a song.'

Fintan gapes, he droops. 'Constructivism,' he says. 'It was the only logic. Where did it go? Fertile once – you don't expect it to go on for ever, people move, they go on foot, on horseback if they can, carry their roof trees, if they ever had them, on a cart, perhaps. Mostly – nothing. Take what you pick up on the way. The lightest knowledge: no banality, no dwelling on weaknesses and pain. Training! You need it, make it your habit. Living on nothing? You have to train....'

We laugh, and Jessica rubs Fintan's jaw, her long dark index like a fireman's oilcan ... coaxing out more distance, more prediction, a frame to set us in. Hers – a gesture of friendship, even love. But none of that is round about.

'Electro's gone, Fintan,' says Jessica, quite gently. 'It took, sprouted, and then – no more. Histories, there were a lot, and they were old, Fintan, very very old in human terms. Things end up here, they take on ancient names, do ancient things. Emirs, that's what flourishes.'

'I realise it's so,' says Fintan. 'If you don't direct the show, you hope it turns out – as something different. But there's a paradox – if it really works – it lasts. Like you say, Jessica – it lasts until it's very very old. It becomes a parasite that smothers its own growth with parasites. They are the strongest things alive – the bugs. People don't realise: that's the war and they're the warriors. We're going under, faster, if we don't see that.'

'You care about it, then,' I say, mocking. 'You're emotional about destiny?'

'More than you'd imagine,' Fintan says. 'It isn't will or instinct – it's commitment. Your energy is what you have, it's everything, and you must use it, all, all the time. If you doubt your reality, Torsten, I'll stick this thorn through your cheek,' and he advances on me – 'So – work on it! We're not scorpions – you mustn't think surviving is why you're here. You can't just sting and sting, then go and sleep in someone's shoe.'

'I didn't know I had to know,' I say. 'Why I am. Long ago, people pestered themselves with that, gave themselves no rest until they had an answer. Now – it's diversification. Speeding up, compressing; and diffusion.'

He doesn't bother telling me that I am trivial. I know. I shouldn't spar with him.

Jessica pulls out the thorn – it didn't go far in.

'What are we doing here, Fintan?' she asks. 'Looking for tall trees?'

'Oh,' he says. 'There are still those!'

'I know you, Fintan,' I say, seeing suddenly – 'You're a True Communist!'

'Maybe, maybe,' he says, smiling and for the first time patting my shoulder in a friendly way – I remember Odette doing that, before my first mission with the renegade Manlio, fixer and enslaver.

The bus exposes your mortality. Also – your motivation – the in-between, the haberdashery of roadscape, ribbons of habitations, weeds: threads pulled. You suffer it because you have the faith; the faith monotony and repetition are not the juice of life. You're wrong. Manlio knows, that when you get off the bus at last, you must go down, be purified, find the guy who blows smoke in your face, brings up your granpa's ghost.

We sit and wait.

In the afternoon, guys come, riggers, setting up a sound stage.

'For me,' Fintan says. 'Music is the most important of the arts. Though it's many arts, of course – tourism, mostly.'

There's much testing of the network – instruments are strummed, people are bussed in. Han Chinese, Germans, Colombians, Karnatakans.... Of course, where they now live – it's possible they could all come from the same place. Naturally – we can't tell. They're too excited to talk to us. A group warms them up – they stand, clap and wave '*Ein, zwei, drei, vier*' – they shout, a song. That's the theme.

'They tested atom bombs right here,' says Fintan, gesturing. 'Now, there's space launch. It takes them time to realise – that "space" means there's nothing there. They shoot them up, the tubes, and down they come – the men and women don't burn up, but they are never like before. Their organs are played out. What do you expect?'

*

'You don't know what to do, Fintan,' says Jessica, in quite a gentle way. 'You don't know what to do, or what to look for....'

'Now,' says Fintan. 'I don't see the future, not at all. There will be futures, naturally – millions and millions of them. But – more, I cannot see or say.'

'You came from here, Fintan,' says Jessica. 'Where the early apples were....'

'They kept the fruit but didn't keep the sin,' says Fintan. 'That was swept away. People on strings of little horses – they took women, sometimes there were children. Men: they always seem more sinful. Mostly, they did not survive, the massacre was like a cure for bad diseases.... They all died, men, children, women too, sometimes everybody died, they always had ... the politics, the temperaments, anger and pride.... The sin was carried westward – it lingered in the marches, in the wetlands of East Poland – there were centres there; you know they can repeat it all....'

'What we can do,' says Jessica, 'we three – is go around. We ask what Fintan asks: "Do we go on, is there continuity here?" If not, then we go on to somewhere else.'

It's as good an idea as anything.

'It's a bad idea, Jessica,' says Fintan. 'Nothing's up to people now.'

We look at white houses, grey slate roofs, brown unkempt cows. Cold flat island: a dialect that scrapes your throat. Unyielding pirates always here, always wanting out.

'Your idea, Fintan,' says Jessica.

'Most places export people, Jessica,' Fintan says. 'They go to boss, in their own way. What do you expect them to innovate?'

'There's sharks and whales,' says Jessica. 'The whales are big and slow, live for centuries, eating crumbs. The sharks – they are voracious, swift. I bet they eat each other when they're not being researched. You want to be a pilot fish, Fintan. They don't exist. There's squiggly opportunists, stripey, dull –

eating the leftovers from the sharks. They don't escort – they follow. Why aren't they eaten? Maybe they don't taste so good. There is no right answer: not for little fish nor for big ones. They travel where they want, and you go too, along with them. Kings, republics and dictators – their eating codes are different, they're different kinds of fish. You eat whatever they don't eat. If there's crisis – sometimes you get over it. Sometimes you evolve – usually you go extinct. That's it. It's life, Fintan.'

'It isn't gold and camels, Torsten,' Fintan says, turning away from her, seeming not to hear. 'It's silver. Camels too. And it isn't us, you, me and Jessica. We don't know something that all the rest don't know. The new turn? Look closely, it's begun already. It's people from the centre: Inner Asians. It always has been. China too. Wasn't it always so?'

*

I come from journey's end. When there's a desert, you have to move about, and if you can, you find the edge and travel far away.

'This little place,' says Jessica, as we watch a guy in russet pants stand in the green road and wave a telephone, trying to catch a voice – 'it has a mafia. They run an organisation here – if you're not in it, you have to leave, like I have....'

'All organisations now,' says Fintan, 'those that the law sets up – they kill lots of people, or pervert them; send messages, confuse, leak chemicals or oil or atoms, spill viruses or news or charity.... The difference is – the criminals, they kill their own. Not many, either. That is not their point. They economise, they tiptoe.

'Armies? They're different too. They are made to kill a mass; the corporations do it naturally, by chance, often quite unplanned and by surprise, lack of foresight; unaware of precedent ... hypocrisy....

'It doesn't attract me, Jessica: not to run a mafia, a camorra with its boasting adolescents ... still less an organisation that covers its dirty deeds with laws. Those corporations make the little things that burn your brains....

'Counsel the leaders? Tell them how to hide, dissimulate, or get away with many murders ... is that what I was born to do?'

'You're without hope, then, Fintan,' Jessica says and turns her back on him. 'What's left is dance.'

'As you had guessed,' says Fintan. 'Take away the rest – vainglory and vanity, the poisons and the threats – and yes: it's dance. You're right. You don't even need to hum a tune. Counting's the best. Or – nothing. Move. Stand still. It's all there is.'

'Banks,' I say. 'Fintan: you left out banks. They're life – they are the light that makes plants grow, jigs up your hormones, the glands that make you point your toes.... They are the sun that ripens, then consumes.'

'You're right, Torsten,' Fintan says. 'They're light and death, alpha and omega. My family learned it much too late.'

*

Jessica puts her hand in his, she and Fintan make a promenade, prepare a sequence, a routine. I am not part of it. It's assertion and defeat.

They don't see me leave.

THE SHIP OF FOOLS

It's a bad time, for me, for everyone. You need to get away, but to be with people. Disaster's all around, but hard to see, to pick it out. Everyone hallucinates.

Everybody has a world within them, what they've been and what they think they know. It's a cabinet of curiosities.

Fintan and Jessica – when they danced off, I thought – 'get away: go somewhere big. Africa. Brazil. A new start in old places that you've always known. Leave the war, take ship – and don't go home. You've no one waiting. Go where people are leaving – there'll be room for you. Go where people look to the north – you, look south. Find a boat that will not sink – that's the most important thing.

I'm the captain. I want to be the captain; why else? Why else embark? All veiled, men and women, whatever they like to call themselves, all veiled, the eyes – especially the eyes: all whirling on the deck. An island? Take ship: – if you don't find a continent, there's islands. The Amazons, the Black Sea folk, the pirates, smiths of every metal ... they sailed everywhere, the world was smaller then. Down below, the heavy silver ticking dynamo goes by itself.

Land ho!

An island...?

Circe's island? For sure it isn't Ithaca.... We avoided that! Magic and sorcerers – a lovely witch – her sun-washed island, well appointed, bars and loungers.... One of the strange sort, where if you land, you are invisible, or have your bones sucked out to give you – a great lightness ... when you're back on board, the cat chases you up and down as if you're feathers, silver feathers. When you see land – it could even be an island. Or it could be Tunisia.

We're fools, of course, that's why they make me captain, I appoint myself ... that's why we're on the ship seeking an eerie island, why we're off and looking for an island we know will make us ... stranger still. An island joined to other lands, strange lands, sorcerers and odalisques ... white horses never ridden, pink houses ... games with unmarked dice.... Time is honey, maybe those strong Cuban bees will sweeten us and slow us down.... It isn't likely. The present will happen faster, and faster still, bringing us together. We're awkward without lookalikes, but we already know it all, present, future. Everything – it shimmers, doesn't last.

The old time stopped after the belle époque, a glory time when we were starved and sick, like we had always been.... We thought the culls would stop. They went on, magnified.

We dance, there's nothing else that brings us so much joy….

Seeing ends of the world, watchtowers abandoned, old news handed out, tacked up on blackboards ... demos, promises and souvenirs? Why not?

Inner Asia? Like Fintan said: Sovetskaya Bukhara: 'fifty years of revolution', going on forever. The paper browning, brittle.

Passport from and to no country. The world has many centres – a big oyster, more centres than the pearls. The Black Sea – where the Amazons came from – if it wasn't Libya. They took ship too, finished in the forests of Brazil.

You take ship – you might reach home, you land in Africa instead. It's so big, all you can see is what you were when you set out.... I wanted to find the place, the right one – the right people. Error after error. Everyone on board a ship expects to find the magic land, it stops you looking at the waves.

The supple Sakine, and all the rest; the dancers in the sealight. Nice 1930. Khiva: opened up and painted by Matisse. Sea-water coming in as strips of coloured foam.

It's very hot. We sweat, no end to our impurities, into the sea.

Remember what no one else can, not ever, and keep it to yourself.

WAFA

She was not Berber.

I don't go for tattoos. She, her boy friend and I, were drunk, they put a red butterfly on my leg, the needle caused it to go varicose and it became an eagle. It looks like a portwine birthmark now.

She wasn't Berber, but she had Berber tattoos, she'd come from France to star in a movie that collapsed, never made, everybody stranded, and the country is not quite an island, though nearly, as the frontiers were all closed. Wafa, she called herself, picked up Ayoub for protection, but he was a padlock on her. She lived in Rouen, said 'Rouyn' like in Québec, explaining where she's from: the song says how I fled being caught with my love in Rouyn, 'with one shoe off and one shoe on'. Just a thought, a bridge, so she and I connect. She's resigned – to years of being shipped around – 'without a ship,' she says, '*capisc*'?'

'Get me a granita, Ayoub!' she says. She dresses sexy, but she doesn't stand out here. Almost everyone is beautiful, in different ways.

Wafa's home.

It's not where I want to be, and they are not the people to be with.

*

Wafa could do anything. She's new, into the old business. Trade, conquest by trade.

All the people I have met are part of something large, elaborate – take them away, the scenery, a portico, falls down. They are taken up, absorbed, by what they do – like a snake becomes its rattle, the butcher – his pig; the warrior – her boots and belt. Elise – is her dark rooms, a suite of them inside.

Jessica – is her arms and legs.

Wafa can bring you complex things – the true religion, pills to drink it down and make it float, a gun to bring up a congregation, and to punish innocence. She doesn't care if you fall off her cart, and a wheel goes over you. She moves. Maybe she can move me with her....

Ayoub clings on.

*

'Be content, Wafa,' I tell her. 'Simplicity. Forget history. You've no career. A career will end, be very difficult. They'll patronise you, cheat you. What you'll value, what you'll remember – is fragments, flashes, not worth writing down. Choose a country that sails close to the wind, a ship without a destination. There is no imperative. No outline, nothing you mustn't cross, nothing that doesn't blow away. Compulsion – will come and often go.... Nothing you do will make a difference. What you think, you cannot shout; it won't be heard, and if it's heard you'll go to jail, for being right, for being wrong. Being good – is only done in silence, unobserved.

'Ayoub is bland. Without him, you'll find other bland possessive people.... Goodness – doesn't work. Being bad – I'll have to stop you....'

'You've got it all wrong,' says Wafa. 'You always do. That's what you've learned: remember, you're always wrong.'

We're sitting in La Samaritaine. Could be Marseille – the movie. Guns, drugs, ships. I'm sure Wafa wants to go to France, get rid of Ayoub.

'We're doing something useful,' Wafa says. 'Trade. Enlightenment. Cash and aspiration. The whole world is down there, underneath our feet.... Invisible roads.'

I say, 'It's a poor world, Wafa. Sand, armed trucks.'

'We start small,' she says. 'We'll be the big dwarves.'

'It's a movie,' I say, still always being wrong. 'You go down south, there's abandoned haciendas, pueblos that can hold thousands – all empty. Movie sets. Then there's desert, full of people with plans you can't imagine. Everyone's a proxy, everyone has a state, a flag, waiting to be unfurled. Except for you. You sell them flags. Then there's the soldiers; and bergs of sand big as Antarctica, flaking off. And you don't know – where the motors head, who thinks what.... People who think we'll all go down to hell for not believing right. Others in hell already.'

'You have to have what people want,' she says. 'That is: you have to sell what people buy.'

'You must *be* people people want,' I say. 'And you'll wear out, as quick as quick.'

'We don't propose to cut you in, Torsten,' she says. 'You're opportunist. You seek the company of sharks and follow them.

They don't need you. You don't taste good – not you, and not your sermons.'

'I am frivolous, Wafa,' I admit.

'I've always had strong faith,' she says. 'And love my countries. You must have both – faith and love.'

'I'm on your side, Wafa,' I say. 'I'm not sure I bring it faith and love – a side, it runs like water. Like sand. You're right: yours, is not a side, it's trade.'

'You must bring enlightenment,' she says. 'You needn't believe in it. Your force is money, not force – people are very poor, Torsten,' she says accusingly. 'It isn't who you save, it's who you kill – that is the test. You sacrifice – it's their salvation. Starting with the animals, then you go up....'

'I know, Wafa, I know. You should keep out of it. Friends are no help, you need lots more than friends,' I say.

'I'm not a friend,' she says.

She'll nest in Lorzot.... 'You had connections, Torsten....' Wafa says, 'The Sahel ... all that.... Big empty places – you're attracted there....'

'Oh,' I say. 'I could organise caravans, that's all. The little ones – they merge with larger ones, until the whole sandscape is moving – tufts of brown on tan....'

'And do they all arrive?' she asks.

'They all have arrived,' I say.

It's a tricky subject, this. Her trades, her deals, her mates, her clan....

*

'I quite misread you, Wafa. I expect everyone I meet to be pristine, just washed up, out of their egg, dropped from a basket....' I tell her. 'It isn't so. I ought to know by now.'

I'm lost. When you're lost, there's nothing, nothing at all, that you can do. Being told exactly where you are – confirms it: you are lost.

*

'There's no use for you, Torsten,' Wafa says. 'You wring your hands, bring out the best in strangers. No use at all. Daring and flexibility – can you give me that? I can't go where you'll have to go, can't make shaky deals and drop them like you'll have to do.... I must be the rock.'

'No,' I say. 'You belong, you're heavy with mortality.... You root.'

'My beauty comes from that,' she says. 'But I'm not supposed to know.'

She looks me over, without interest. 'I have what people want,' she says. 'I *am* what people want. I can give anything – teachers and missionaries, sacrifices, warriors, mediators, illuminators, mechanics and carpenters. Everybody sees – I have the faith, and I am not afraid, I'm not like you, I value riches, excavations – kids sent down holes, and crane-drivers. Butchers and cowherds, Torsten. I know how it works, all of it, even when it seems that nothing works at all, I can supply. That is the trick, that's what makes it all go on. When you are writing "End", I'm at the beginning ... that wheel with many spokes, round and round it goes, and people trust me, they like me. While you're adrift, Torsten, looking for your happy place, I'm in my warehouses full of boxes that I stole....'

'I know, Wafa,' I say. 'People need those boxes. You'll get them on a truck, I'm sure.'

She doesn't seem to hear: 'God wants what I do,' she says. 'God – He's a crook, a bit of a crook, like me. Otherwise it wouldn't all turn out right, just like He wants. And just think of it – all those people that He kills, each day, before the dawn, the coffins and the tears that must be made, according to what's in the book – armies destroyed without a trace, diseases inflicted, plagues contrived, species exterminated, kingdoms dissolved and daughters raped – all so that in the end, His will is done and it will turn out just exactly as He wants. And I am His right arm, and He will cut it off the moment that He wills.'

'Why not?' I ask. 'Why not?'

I work it round, what she has said, trying to domesticate the thought. 'So, if there was not God, making it all in time come out – all would be up to you. To me....'

'Yes,' she says. 'To you and me and Ayoub. And Ayoub's prick. And all our vanity.'

Well, yes, of course, it would be up to everything, to everything and everyone that we can see.

PEOPLE WHO HAVE STORIES

Tunisian women – women in Tunisia – they are remarkable. Wafa – will have a full story you can tell.

The others – Elise, Jessica – they have, they are, excerpts. Paragraphs, a few sentences. Elodie – she's like Wafa, with a full, a shapely, story.

Encountering these stories – you don't come out well, Torsten, I warn myself. You don't come out at all, you haven't enetered in. It's good. Better not.

Wafa's a killer. Never in person.

She runs a network, she'll make states made of ropes with slipknots. Places that make me, make everybody, suffer, set the teeth in acid: Mali, Niger, Burkina. They use lots of magic, they need it, there's never enough, not nearly.

Wafa won't be visible. She'll contrive, conspire: the result is painful. Send in the white gods! Soldiers.

The people she kills are real, not ghosts. There's nobody can stop her, or those like her.

She sends her trucks into that huge populated space, the vast desert and the vaster metaphor. It's not an island, she's not Circe.

*

Odette – some wandering god has turned her, like a Daphne, into a flowery block. Elise has made her bucks squeezing emotions no one has, from her banalities: the cloudy ruined 'scapes where we all must live.

Down with them all, and down with me for harbouring them, for sharing their biology.

Shame! Shame on the indifferent who submit, shame on the slavers.

Pity the illusion of escape!

INTERESTING AND UNLIKELY

'I trust you, Manlio,' I say. 'I have a mission, and you're the person....'

'... most likely to do it for you,' says Manlio. We laugh.

'Wafa,' he says, 'is the most intriguing and unlikely person you have met. Those fractured tribes and clans, the big ideas in slippery hands, big ignorant powers returning to mess things up again – it's a great story, but.... You won't make sense of it. It's not been making sense for centuries, accumulating layers of no sense.... Time going on, like it must, people are born and pray and feed their animals, have kids, all just improvised to make a killing or a meager profit ... and here's another player.... Wafa, in the wrong place with unconfessed ideas ...Pills, guns and faith; soldiers and mines.

'It all turns out banal, I'm sure. A trucking business ... transports everyone and everything.'

'I want to see design,' I tell him.

'Pattern?' he asks. 'There's always those. Repeat a figure. But, Torsten – you are mistaken. You stand – your mind's a promontory – you look out. But – everybody has one, a look-out, vantage-point: identical. We all stand, look out. We're gulls – we use the rocks as places where we breed and then take off in flight. Your mind, your rock – you want to stay there. It's a mistake. You even think it moves, is a vessel, sails or boiler maybe. It's not so. You've nothing smart to say, and you won't leave the topic and keep quiet.

'We're wrong to team together. You're the tearful type, Torsten.'

'It's Time, Manlio,' I say. 'When it's present, there is sadness. A fear of falling, that feeling of vertigo.... That's the small, most innocuous part of it.'

'Your worldview, Torsten,' says Manlio, picking an argument, 'gets in the way. Besides, the missions that you set yourself are miscalled. What you have is curiosity.'

'You think you see clearly, Manlio?' I ask, as he rubs steam from the bus window.

'Alas,' he says. 'The days of mercenaries are coming to an end. Fixers and messiahs, like I can be – we're losing out, The powers that matter – they'll decide how to manipulate a future. We who train, put others under fire – all that will pass. The grey stream will set, in what it is – cement.

'And you, Torsten – your scenery, the quotes, nostalgia, little tunes that roam inside your head – those will become antiquities. *Tout passe!* my friend. The new order will come.

'You think we're taking risks and making history? To all the others on the bus – we're two gays on holiday. You've taken a lifetime proving that you're straight. Others more adaptable ... a week in college gives more thrills and tears than you have ever had....'

'Yes, Manlio,' I say. 'You're right. Survival – that's the prize, and everyone who lives will find it handed to them grudgingly – a leaking chalice, tacked together from recycled junk....'

'You have avoided, Torsten,' Manlio says. 'Following the people you have met, into the extremities: their failures, degradations, physical dissolutions you so fear for yourself.

And yet – they're on the edge, you leave them there, but there's no doubt at all that they will fall. You don't describe it, but you know, we know – it will not end at all in a good way.'

'A precious insight, Manlio,' I say.

I'd not suspected it. But, yes – I leave them, friends, lovers, comrades – when their infection, their destiny, is just about to show itself in trembling and sweat: I tiptoe out.

*

'This place,' says Manlio, trying to stretch himself in the small seat designed for economies of space and people much much shorter, thinner, than he is – pointing at the scene that speeds away, 'is like all places on the brink of dissolution. The ancient ways are exposed and swept away. Or – everything's just buried, these low compounds, suburbs unending, pseudo-cities that live by fish and coconuts or combing wool from goats and suchlike – places that should not exist, places that do not exist, and yet they stretch through universes imagined, filled with unimaginable creatures. Interminable Senegals, the *griots* recount them, dramatise and picture them and print them out like playing cards, arrange them into epics or set them in sand, in mandalas....'

'Extremes, Manlio?' I ask, bristling. 'Moralities? You mean Elodie? Your behaviour quite inexcusable and not excused, one day it will collapse back on you. Elodie, ending in torture, prison, betrayal ... your venality to blame....'

'Feuds? Vendettas, *faide*, Torsten?' he asks. 'That is how life has always been. The feuding ties you down, so you take ship to get away. Find slaves: people to rob. Every ship – a space ship, cramped and smelly, every camel a space capsule, rumbling gas, up high and higher ... the exploration, finding people as strange and ordinary as we are ourselves. The explorer – is extraordinary, finding ordinary people set in their ordinariness. But the explorer – she's us! The extremes are ours, further and further out we go, and there we are, teetering into plague pits, gathering under scaffolds ... watching the processions in the skies, millions of demigods each with their woody duplicate – a branch, a tree-root – casually protecting us, our candle, and our ox....

'We are made to betray, destroy. That is exploration, Torsten. A dirty precarious trade. There's the golden queen? – you melt her down. That's what the two of you are made for....'

No one can respond to that.

*

New scenes, glimpsed through the opacity – our humid breaths.... You need new words, and we can't think of any. Invent them – no one understands.

'You don't imagine, Torsten, little man,' says Manlio, brooding. 'That when we find what we may never find – you'll take it out on me, for Elodie? Vengeance will be yours? I can't imagine that.'

'No one tells you to,' I say. 'That's genre. This isn't genre.'

*

I hear 'nip nip' from the seat behind. 'Mind the copperhead,' says a voice, and some fingers prod me through the iron frame of my seat. A snakehead.

‘Don’t take anything from them,’ says Manlio. ‘It’s shit.’

‘I don’t use,’ I say.

‘Then you’re a real *pédo,*’ says Manlio, turning, grinning and saying no with his head to the guy behind. ‘We’re eagles,’ he says to me. ‘We eat copperheads. I do, anyway. You discriminate,’ he says to me. ‘Because you’re squeamish, not because you are a connoisseur. And politics too,’ he says. ‘With you – there is no peace, I know. Nothing curious, revealing, impresses you. Volcanoes don’t impinge.... Just business, never done.’

We go much higher, the windows clear. Outside, there’s shepherds. It’s guerilla country. Not for me. Already I feel the air thin, the engine misses, we all contemplate mortality.

‘It’s the paradox of paradise,’ I tell Manlio. ‘Higher and higher – you’re in heaven, it’s so high there’s no oxygen, and so you die....’

He doesn’t laugh.

‘You’re no theologian, Manlio,’ I say. You don’t see the funny side.’

*

‘I pity you, Torsten,’ says Manlio. ‘Your world of left and right, liberals, conservatives – all that will go. Has gone. Your irrelevance: you see it as resistance, independence. Most people in the future are irrelevant, and they sing your song. It’s like a hatch of turtles – all alike, each weaker, stronger, than the next, luckier or sadder. Some few get to the sea. The new order won’t bother with you. It will be one world, but how far will the parts go to keep their privileges and their interests?

Will they do deals or skirmish? Cage you? Risk the next big bang?'

'Stasis? Hostilities?' I ask. I've no idea.

'Invent, Torsten,' says Manlio. 'Try to analyse. Be careful. Use your imagination, don't congeal. Marx started off with movement, destruction, dynamism and constant change. Then he discovered economics, became granitic, wrote those awful books. Full stop. Then Terror, wars – order and slavery. Him – a name, one of the many many names of god: irrelevant, an incantation. Rockets and deserts – those go strong! This, what were in, might as well be the last bus.'

'Futures are always different,' I say. 'And so are we.'

'China,' says Manlio. 'Only in China does someone think. They take the risk – it must be worth it, so it's done. What? What do they think? How should I know – I'm here. What effect will it have? I've no idea. It's all there is. Probably useless. Analysis – it doesn't change a thing. It doesn't matter, none of it, not to me. I know you're sentimental about thinking, Torsten, though yours – doesn't impress. Your musings are the usual: – a cabinet of curiosities. You're ignorant. Last century. What do you trust? Hands and feet, showdowns and showing-off.

'You know the last century was disastrous – so, go back another hundred years. See if that will put it right. It's pitiful! and now you want revenge on me for Elodie?'

'It isn't why we're here,' I say. 'Not to put things right.'

'Still further back?' he asks. 'Why do you need me?'

'Not starting over, Manlio,' I say. 'No regrets, no separations. But you've a hard, a sceptic's, head. You will survive, you'll be a pioneer.

'Poor Elodie ... it's always death or compromise. No hard feelings, Manlio....'

He doesn't hear.

*

The track is basalt. We're at the top. There's clouds, and there's a sign. 'Completion of the Species Project.' 'Human: all human to 100%.'

'We've found it, Manlio,' I say.

*

I make the driver stop – we're at the crest. Ahead there is a palisade, armed guards outside. Some beautiful people looking out, quite blank. Were they grown here? Did they apply?

'We go in here,' I say to Manlio – he says:

'No, no – this place is not for us. It's where our species occupies the last wild spot, and here we celebrate supremacy. All other animals are for our pleasure or our use. To watch or milk, then eat. Well done! – a spectacle in life and death....'

'That's food for thought,' I say.

*

'This place,' says Manlio. 'It looks as if it's primitive – experiment without convenience....

'I'm a cosmopolitan – this to me is punishment.... Then there's your mission, Torsten. What of that...?'

'We all have missions, Manlio, many in our lifetime, mostly not performed, forgotten or impossible.... Some after death propose to go to hell or paradise,' I say. 'Now, *you* are my mission. Once it was Elodie, she is no more, our mission to her was blundered through, and void. You take her place now....'

I step back – it's not in Manlio's character to run or fade away.... He stays.

My exit route is free.... Too bad for him.

'This,' shouts Manlio, 'is not commensurate.... Not justice, not approximate. You set those guards on me? Part of your fantasy there's guilt in preservation of oneself; as if survival's not our primary goal....'

'Nothing is commensurate,' I shout back to him. 'A justice done – appears as random, disconnected from the flow, an accident, a mishap, like a rare disease that drops on you without just cause....

'The guards? People are kept out, or they're allowed in. Selection's never just. Beware, regret that you're a specimen that wins respect. This is the victory of civilisation, Manlio. It's tough. *You're* tough. *Zivilisation,* Manlio, and not *Kultur*: that's you.

'They'll want you, to keep you, for your dimensions regular, your values universal, universally compromised. They'll keep me out, I'm weedy, unsuccessful and depressed. Free radical who's self-obsessed....

'The vengeance: it isn't mine, it's Elodie's. Of course, she will not know – perhaps she wouldn't even want....

'Civilisation's mine as well, my destiny. I've nothing, nowhere else. The world is civilised, and culture snaps at it, to bring it down. The civil – it's the best that we can do. We're more inventive than the dinosaurs, less finely tuned than humming birds, connecting worse than whales.... I'm in the species, you can see. Not a good example, though. We've won, we're everywhere: we cage, we eat, the animals. To be consistent, though, we have to cage ourselves.

'You'll start here, my friend; without machines. Here, there's no nature, only clouds – you'll have to make a nature by yourself. You'll invent. You'll cage and eat, invent machines that do the work for you, then you'll import more people, they'll do the work that machines can't, and you don't want to do....

'It's vanity, and we are vain.... You'll think you're on the way to something higher, more complete and radiant – but no, my friend: that's it. That's life....'

*

Manlio's a feline, a fine predator – and I'm the croc who's nervous, restless in the noontime heat, don't close an eye, drift out where the water's deep, too deep for pussy to pursue....

*

A guard takes him inside – they keep you in, they keep you out.

It's neat, but it's not an ending.... Manlio will get to be a guard, talk himself out.

The people-farm itself will fail and close: it's too harsh and exposed up here.

The future is not this, maybe.

*

I trudge on down the descent. I'll hear the bus behind....

*

I got beaten really bad. If Manlio had been with me, they'd probably have held off.

*

Violence is different in city and village, best keep on the move between them. It's luck. Being beaten, left for dead, and all the time you're alive!

I was lucky – Nour patched me, she needn't have, not being professional. It wasn't difficult, and besides, a man being knuckled, kicked and stoned, is old history. But not that old – there's been a progress. No mutilation, no feet cut off, all over in a few minutes, no trauma, no rape, no childhood threatened, no relatives involved....

'You've got ideas about history and ceramics, and God and space,' says Nour. 'But you know, Torsten, no one is interested. Not just they don't remember what you think, and try to sort it out. Even if they could remember it – people would not be interested.'

'I know,' I say. 'Many of the people that I've known – they just went off somewhere, ceased to exist. For me, at least. Elise, for instance. Has a reputation, up there with other names you wouldn't recognise. But, forget the reputation, and she's dull, confused. Creative? Confused, that's how she reaches novelty....'

'I've more bad news,' she says. 'You move around, Torsten, and it's good. Other people – they fall off the hill – you don't, and you don't even push them, just let them lose their balance ... or have trouble with their brains. But my news is – that I'm in love with someone else. I don't see him, not any more, haven't seen him for years, but he takes up all my loving room.'

'I don't care too much about you, Nour,' I say. 'Besides, my time is limited. It's an anomaly – Time ... the one thing about it, is it isn't limited. But for me it is. For you, it doesn't seem to be. For you, time's like money: if there's no more gold, you can strike up shells, or lead. For me – time is savings. They go, go quick, and you're unemployed, probably for ever.'

'You should be thinking, Torsten,' says Nour. 'Think Chinese. Don't worry about love – it doesn't need an object, it's what you feel yourself. Enjoy it or get rid of it. More important – is your thought. Your suffering's a bore, a hindrance. Don't let it in.'

'I need more help than that,' I say.

This conversation – it's ridiculous.

'I'll help you cross the river, Torsten,' she says. 'You might manage it. Remember – you cross the river using stepping stones. We're stepping stones, Torsten. We don't cross.'

'I know about women, Nour,' I say. 'I don't know what to do. Without a boat – I have to use you stepping stones ... I know.'

'You said the word,' she says. 'Boat. You could make one. Even if you don't know how.'

We leave it there.

*

'You talk too much of "everything", Torsten,' says Nour. 'It's a way of saying "nothing". Like justice is replete with "injustice" – and so, and so. The people you've been with, didn't tackle everything. They're not like you. They tried to do "something". They walked a stretch with you – and off they go! Managing! They've no time for you.... You're not a danger, you don't resolve. You don't expose what's to be done.'

'Stay, Nour,' I say. 'I'm lucky. Lucky with money – it comes to me, I lose it, everybody does, everybody who's lucky, gets it, loses it. I should have bought from those guys, although I said I didn't use. They rolled me, beat me, didn't find the money: mine and Manlio's.... I keep it in my shoe – they didn't look, they thought it was too obvious I guess.'

'Everybody puts it there,' she says. 'I found it.'

'Stay, Nour,' I say.

I'm all smashed up inside. It hurts – that's good, you know what has to cure.

'Show some humanity,' I say. 'It's happened to me, disaster. It is the time for comradeship.... You'll have your chance. Give me a hand, you'll be rewarded, probably: ten times more wealth and happiness....'

'I told you, Torsten,' says Nour. 'I love someone else.'

'You won a hand,' I say. 'That was your luck. You cashed in too quick. I had – I am – a broken flush. If you go off, I'm sorry for you – and myself, naturally, as well. But – it's nothing, you've only picked up crumbs. You've settled for a part, and that's quick gone.'

'There's nothing we can do,' she says. 'I took some care of you. That's it!'

'Chance, Nour,' I say. 'A fleeting passage. It proves nothing.'

'You're a mixture, Torsten,' says Nour. 'But not of everything. You're not emblematic. Some – many – things you cannot be, cannot believe, nor disbelieve; experience, forget, regret. Your idea, your purpose – it's flawed before it is announced. It's cloudy chapters. Post-stations of the imagination, new teams of horses every dawn.'

'Faith, love, death – you can't drag those along,' I say. 'Not on a mission. A person's just merely a poor sod, fallen off the cart. What you believe – doesn't matter, not a bit. Faith, love, death: we're democratic, you don't need any of that stuff....'

'I have all those, Torsten,' she says. 'I've had them since my birth. I've always been the best.'

'Anyway,' I say, 'mine's not a mission. It's my attempt to understand it all. Then, maybe, make a choice. For that it doesn't make a difference, what you are, what century you're in, what mode of thought.... Anyone can choose.'

*

There's always clouds round here. It's good – it means there's weather; rain and sun.

'Try to stand, Torsten,' she says.

I'm lame. Both legs.

'Try to speak, Torsten,' she says.

The words are there, all in a heap, like in a dictionary, some pictures too, *santini,* icons, bodhisattvahs on horses, always white, the talismans they sell for pilgrims ... karmic merit, that is what I need. The words spill out, like salmons' entrails.... Words jump and skitter – slippery fish that break a surface, then fall back.

Aphasia can be artistic, like Odette's. Mine is like Babylon, the tower.... Immigrants, their cheap labour ... that cramped impoverished city, so vainglorious ... but how to leave the anthill if you're an ant? Did you leave the city every day, go to work the fields, those broken sickles, clay, discarded? Or did you have to stay within the walls, paying taxes, getting sick? Slaves? Or short-term sweats?

*

Language. If you're not a pro, writing it down, nothing you say has ever any impact. You're with the rest of us, merely a speaker, words like falling leaves. What moves the clock forward is your death. You call that resonance? I don't think so. Anything written down, even in good paint on a porous wall – can be erased, but doesn't die. If you just talk, every day, all your life – it's nothing. Seasons, life and death, that's all. Talking, living – it's just a part of death and friendship, leaving people, other people of all sorts, leaving them behind, or seeing them go first – it's having the time of your life. Those thousands of messages on a screen – it's illusion. They don't count, not at all.

That was yesterday. People say there were books then, they don't remember bonfires. Anyway, I wasn't there.

Service, humanity – patching up a chancer like me. It's beautiful. She's an angel: Nour. Leave me, I'm incurable. Well or ill, it's much the same – for you, Nour. Not for me....

*

'I'm not equipped for you,' she says. 'You're very sick. I stole your money, Manlio's too. It doesn't count – I'm sure you're straight, both of you. If there's no romance – it's only cash. I'll name one of my children after you. Whatever I don't need, I'll give it to the cause.'

'You're on the right track, Nour,' I say. 'I'm not even starting out.'

'You must decide, Torsten,' she says. 'When you look in the sky, maybe see a pale pale Jupiter – is that life? Or are your crutches life? Your life?'

These questions – they are excellent. I'm in callipers, I'm off the straight, I tack and go about, I'm like a crab.

They map my brain – put me in a pod – they don't find anything. No thought, no memory, and no anomalies. As Nour said, we're democrats, we start with heads stuffed with a porridge, a polenta, manioc, dal, depending where we're from, it seems and then, there's the piano lesson.

'Attempt an architecture,' the teacher says. 'Progressions, that make sense at any speed. Touch the piano, feel that it responds – it is your interlocutor. It won't repeat what you are doing – come towards it – you are different creatures – you're the lion and it's the alligator – you must live together in your place, the wet, the dry, the cool, the torrid....'

All the familiar notes are there – with little effort you can repeat the past and sketch a future – or they can re-tune it, your comrade, have her sing to any scale or none, respond to any thought you have or metaphor.... She won't repeat. There's sequences, but nothing is sequential. You're in among the trees, and sometimes you're not there at all, for years and years.

'I can't do it,' I tell the teacher. 'Not at all. I understand you, but I don't communicate, the keyboard's something I can't recognise, not me, not anyone I've ever known. I don't respect the difference, it and me, because I don't know what it is. To me, the instrument should be my voice. It isn't so, you say: it's argument, materials....'

'I'm not a teacher, Torsten,' says the woman. 'I tell you what's to know. The instrument is not your voice – it's a response. It answers what you say, if it can grasp your argument. It recognises statements, metaphors, and any kind of curlicue of phrase or logic, algebra or pulse....'

'And meaning?' I ask. 'I might think I have a question or an insight – want to play it out.... Does the instrument have understanding? Does it complete my thought, my intuition? Follow it, add to it? Does it have a discourse it is master of? Present it in a dialectic with me, or is it quite autonomous. And then – who knows? Who understands anyway....'

'Oh well,' the lady says, 'it won't play by itself. It is an instrument, you're present, naturally, but the music – is it in you? Or in the strings? My notion is it has to be in both of you, but that it can't be separate, you can't say "I'm the music", and the strings can't say, "No, no – it's me."'

'I understand,' I say. 'But to me – I have a life the instrument can never have, initiatives, ideas and questions, compositions no piano has. It's mute. A spokeshave isn't full of chair-legs, a piano's similar – a sonata starts and finishes in me – it passes through the instrument, and that is it. If I'm not there – not only there's no music – there's no sound, no movement.... The lid is down.'

*

'You're full of prejudice, Torsten,' she says. 'You toy with images of slavery, of ancient horrors, empires, patriarchs and matriarchs – you look for hierarchy, for being in control, a boss. I fear your brain is shot....'

'Maybe I can't do what you want, means I can do it in a hundred different ways,' I say.

I'm desperate.

'I'm cured,' I tell her. 'Now, tell me what I had?'

'They beat you up,' she says. 'It makes no difference. Your condition – the quests, the judgements – all is false. You are disordered, Torsten. I'd say "start again" – but there's no start, nowhere you can begin that would imply an end. It's you, what you have made, derived a picture that you set before reality. Remember Elise – she took her picture from reality, then scumbled it – at least she understands where she is placed.... You think you have the power.... Your brain should tell you that it isn't so....'

'But – where the species stands – it is disastrous,' I say. 'We fucked it up.... Millions....'

'Your time is nearly up,' she says. 'I have more gifted aspirants: outside, there is a line of people more *sympa*. Your woman has to pay me, only me. There was no cure for all the rest, your ills, your absent friends. Remember what I tried to tell, and try to understand, at least appreciate, the music. Find a place that's safe and stretch out with your claws, your callipers, listen and enjoy....'

I say, 'You haven't faced my question: what's to be done, what can I do...?'

And the despair ... it makes me weep, I can't repair the damage anyone has done, not that I've done anything, I've not begun.... And I am broken now.

Outside, the corridor is full of children, some are very young, and all are beautiful – they talk together about space and physics, life in those ancient cities, forced labour on the towers and in the fields....

I ought to tell them to beware, and not to trust.... Perhaps they know, but I can't speak to them, their conversation is beyond me, my personality broken, my voices multiple and false....

*

'Are there so many, so many young people, with damaged brains, waiting in this corridor, for lessons I myself cannot assimilate?' I ask aloud.

'It doesn't show till later,' says a guy, smoking a joint, wearing a white coat down to his boots. 'All animals are cute when they are young – then they grow a shell or claws, or fangs, or stinky glands beside their arse. And you, my friend –

be careful. You are badly broken – your brain's regressed. Don't think it's positive. You're chipped and swollen. Do you want to go back, back where you were before, when this disaster hadn't happened yet, but now you know it will?'

'I realise that,' I say. 'We are all sick, that's why we die. The span is short.'

'The problematic lies,' the whitecoat says – and is he doctor, porter, or gravedigger? – in none or all of these?... 'Between the preparation and the destination. Grasp that, and your life becomes direct. Not easier. Not successful. Prepare and aim, Torsten.'

'But....' I begin.

'No,' he says. 'I didn't either. I'd no idea; like you....'

RECRUITING

I need a crew – I need to find the force of nature: of water, and myself ...

... what's passive, what's unstoppable, what makes waterfalls: makes bad spirits and the signs you draw in red upon your cheeks to keep them off.

... otters, monkeys, eagles. All about them.

People of all sorts, wandering, long before my origins and yours. How far they've got, and if there's been anywhere for them to go.

We'll make a movie: we'll lay down some memories. It doesn't mean a thing, but it must stop others coming after, killing everything.

It won't, won't change anything.

Do I need a crew for that? A crew of crows – carousing, corrupting ... cawing.

*

Casually, passing time. Being interviewed for the biggest trip: the river. Four of them, hunching on their stools.

Bar dello Sport.

Cyril, Stivelle, Lucien and Leos.

Stivelle, 'brown and sweet as Belgian chocolate,' says Lucien, his face a sharkskin, gunpowder affliction, a pointillisme of black pepper stops, picked up in Cayenne, where he met Cyril, who's an emaciated know-all, colonial doctor, a diplomatic type, a drifter, with no urge. To him, we're all big dogs – he tots up our chance of years, of a good senility. Part-time barman – he'll be your consultant, your cosmologist.

He's found the way.... Keep us on his lead.

Leos, the Czech sailor with the lantern jaws; a passport that's not his. And me. That's five. All heating up. It's after time, the barman's on his tiptoes: 'home' he thinks. There's no other roisterers, pioneers. He hates us foreigners, but he needs the trade.

*

Have them fight – fight like the old-time gladiators, with salamis and breadsticks. Lucien: he'll win. Condemned when his flintlock exploded. Vengeance not his – the prey fled, bounding off. He is the strongest, but....

*

'The Essequibo river,' Cyril says. 'In Guyana; it has everything – meanders, rapids, falls, sinks, and spume: uncertain beginnings and an end in the effacing ocean: a delta of fat fingers.... All starting as a puddle, a vague intention. The meaning must be immense: it isn't needed, the river has it, keeps it to itself: can decide which is its start and where it ends. A mystery. You can make it yours.'

'It's all known,' says Leos. 'It's been made into a movie we've all seen.... That's how *you* know, Cyril. Knowledge is like that – it's what everybody knows.... People you see every day. Even if you were born naked on the bank, that way, you'd know nothing by yourself, or for yourself. But you'll pick up what everybody else has known. All the knowledge you will need. Journeying, sailing – it's inconsequential. Seeing everything; enabling nothing. Being – that's knowing. Watching, keeping a lookout.'

'You can't avoid,' says Stivelle, 'knowing things that don't fit anywhere.' She spins away from us, carefully tipsy, uses the drink to travel far, say what can't be challenged. 'We should cancel history – except it's always cancelling itself, quite independent of us, but we're there, we're characters upon its stage. On it goes, it all happens simultaneously: everything does. What is, what was. Who's dead – has not existed: is gone utterly, and lives eternally – somewhere. Unknowable. If it doesn't exist today, it didn't exist then, you can be sure. You've no idea – what it was then, what it is now – the ties, the connections – fallen into voids for ever.'

*

Carrying the boat over the mountain, round the falls. A difficult portage. It's a tree, a burnt-out trunk. Stivelle – could cut a path. Maybe they won't succeed. Leave it! They'd have to find a tree the other side – taking four people paddling, one to give commands. Gutting the trunk. Waiting till the embers cool.

*

'You haven't understood the argument,' says Lucien. 'It's better that we think all knowledge is innate. It's much much bigger than what the tribe knows, or our clan. Science: you remember the mistakes, incompetent researchers! Centuries to get it right. But we know it, it knows us. Already, all of it, from the beginning. We know the universe, we're part of it. We know it like the toe knows the knee. The brain's the tiny mirror, a lens, fly's eye of the universe. Each of us has one, identical. Each of us may disappear, and that's too bad. The brain, our standard issue, has seen the universe, understood ... knows how it works, what is infinity, eternity, creation. We don't know what it means, of course, nor what use the knowledge is. We can conceive, embrace and judge, that's all. It doesn't mean a thing, except – that it's what it is.'

*

They're all shouting – I'm shouting at them. So exasperating.

*

We're all quite drunk: I'm looking for a place to go – Guyana isn't it, I am convinced. I know about the spider monkeys and the spiders, the toucans hunting parakeets, each smart creature lurking, preying – quick black eyes like needles keeping everyone sewn, exactly, into the tapestry. The struggle – avails precisely nought. It keeps you where you have to be. However quick and camouflaged you are – you end up in your niche – except....

'Except,' says Leos, 'for catastrophes, which happen regular as night.'

'Everything that is, contains its opposite, its contradiction,' Stivelle says. 'Death holds resurrection. Enslavement – implies a liberation. The river empties, fills. Dry canyon: spate. I'm me, not me, a slave and free, I'm me and everyone, person and number, foetus and skeleton. What I was, I am, and what I might be. Poor and rich: my debt is credit....'

'Yes,' says Lucien. 'Being alive and dead we should be beyond fear and punishment....'

'I know about the river,' I say. 'I know who swims in it, who fishes, who poisons and who purifies. What will happen? It could disappear, who knows. The future's quite inexistent.... Does living tell us anything? Anything it's worth to know?'

*

They don't understand. I don't want to take them anywhere. It's to see if they have been somewhere; have they walked from end to end, from start to start, at the source, when water comes up through the grass from nowhere, starts to flow – to when it disappears into the sea. Enlighten me!

*

'What do you think, Torsten?' I ask myself, since no one else does.

The barman fears the blacks, even those of us who've gone white or whitish, as if we've boiled our skins in caustic. He's suspicious. 'Suppose one day, no drinkers leave the bar?' he asks himself – and he'd be here for ever, serving.

Fascism: in this bar, it smells of streaky underwear, of oft-fried oil. A smell that never goes away, said Elodie.

The animals we've talked about: – just food. Disfigured cuts, pressed and homogenised. Here, in a glass case. Humans eating their way through nature, like in Paris, or in Tokyo – a whim, a wager. Can we eat the world? You bet. Who'd pay out? Generals and ministers, serves them right. And we serve them.

We regress: dividing into wolves and sheep. This country will consume you. Bar dello Sport. Puts you in a pack, or in a flock, then nature takes control. It's hunger rules here. Elsewhere it's muscles.... Pirates from Frisia and Tripoli, always looking for stout oarsmen. When your slaves aren't chained to their bench, there's good chance they will knock you down.

*

The mood's not good. They've done their best. Everything they knew ... and how they knew it. It was mediocrity.

*

'All of you,' I say, 'Have different extreme views. It is good. I am extreme. You can't have enough of them, extremes. Departures, destinations. Living's the extreme we live in. Every time you climb a stair a slip – could be your last. Your time has no duration.

'I'm sure the truth would be extreme, if ever you might come on it....'

*

'When do we start?' asks Leos.

'The right crew, the destination that will fit,' I say. 'How do we know?'

I've no cash, no boxes. No carriers.

'I'll pay another round, and leave you with it here,' I say.

*

'What's money to you, Torsten?' Hari, my fixer, asks.

They call such persons, Hari too, 'guardian angels'. They protect the innocent adventurers. He succeeds Manlio, who I betrayed: his angel wings were plucked, the white feathers went into devils' pillows. When he flaps off bald, look out below! ... be very careful, everyone....

'It's a river,' I say. 'My mission. It's the Essequibo. It links to all other rivers, joined together by their tails. It moves, sometimes it goes underground, or falls off ledges, turns blue or black. It becomes the ocean of all oceans – our wealth, our treasure, capital. Can't drink the sea. You can sail on it – and you don't leave a trace, a track.

'Can those four who answered to my ad, can they make a crew? Explore? The impressive one was Stivelle. Her theory is: there isn't one, no theory. All happens all the time. Presentism, immediacy. You're here – and then you're not, not ever, beyond material, like clouds and beyond them, into a dusty sky....

'The rest had vague ideas about duration, destiny, and memory. Good time and wasted time. Money.... That just flows, and goes to make a single sea....'

'Where's Stivelle from?' asks Hari.

'Africa. Martinique? Or Guadeloupe? A place they don't have rivers, Hari. But they've water all around,' I say. 'The point is – without water – we all die, die on our backs, like all those animals, our white ribs pointing upwards. If you believe in God, that's what you must hope to do ... your bones are indexes, a quantity, pointing in homage to the sky.

'Nature, cash – they must be life. It's written, like the revelation, orienting all you do. Once struck, now printed, as dollar bills, in bills of way, and promissory notes. In the end, the cash must be materialised, so it can be reborn. You have to metamorphose it – build bridges with it, or a courthouse.'

'So,' says Hari, 'money is not a river. Capital – is not the sea. Cash is not life.'

'Think, Hari,' I say. 'There's oceans of it, wealth. If we're not there, the water flows. No one is rich for ever, but the river lives.... And if all rivers die – it's over. That's the end.'

'I shan't give you cash, my friend,' says Hari, not quite following me.

*

'What I really understand,' I say, 'is geography. How do we divide up territory, have people different live side by side – not happy, but, possibly, not murderous? Their skin, their faith, and what they eat.... The songs, divinities, the totems: find them a plot, and have them settle, make what they can....'

'The world partitioned into cultures, more or less?' he says. 'It wouldn't work, and it must not. Think civilisation, Torsten. That, you could boast about. Beware. You put on metaphors when you wake: they are your uniform. You've pips and stripes – no one salutes.

'Dividing people won't bring happiness and peace – it never has. Putting them together? Who can tell?'

'I mean well, Hari,' I say. 'Seeking justice, reason. It's folly, but I feel the innocence of forest folk might be preserved. Maybe I'm out of phase. *Zivilisation,* modernity – it kills, explodes. And it is everywhere. There's not much *Kultur* left. I don't expect to find a lot, however hard I look – and I'll look everywhere.

'I'm reduced to teaching people how to live.... Did they forget? Am I a holy fool? Science and statistics: they made each person count as one, under the same laws of counting and of having cash, dying, having stuff. We lost the other modes of thinking – hunting, magic, fear and reason. We are our naked solitary thing: it's not just capitalism makes us so. And exploration – like a scientist, we put our index into lives ... from curiosity, not love or hate.... Is the river a machine? A teacher?

'Lessons for life. How strange, how ordinary.

'Lucien's too strong, he will get beaten up. The penal settlement, *Strafkolonie*, teaches you to lose. Leos doesn't care, and Cyril's sure he knows it all. Stivelle – I could work on her; she hasn't got a clue....'

'It's important work, Torsten,' Hari says, trying not to laugh: 'Yes. 'How to live', by Torsten – all you need to know. It's good. It's peppy, even.

'Except – you think: partitions. That knowledge you say you have – it's dangerous. You think of keeping people separate – people aren't made for that, and when they are distinct and mingle with their stronger friends – they end up crushed. History, Torsten – it doesn't die, and knowledge isn't innocent. Nothing, no one, is. Your river....'

Hari is ignorant. He comes from somewhere there are rivers – but they're sacred, seasonal. Mostly – they're sand and straw. He lacks my vision.

He's administering Odette's last cash – she being locked like Daphne in her tree.

'I know,' I say. 'Mostly – it's deserted. Water in a ditch. No one wants it.... It's a splendour....'

'Don't be naive,' says Hari. 'People are everywhere – gold, coal, water, oil – it's all riches, everything is dangerous. You're a shell, Torsten – put you in a cannon ... you'll go "bang" ... all smoke!'

ENCHANTMENT

‘What are your skills, Stivelle?’ I ask.

‘Short-order cook, like almost everyone,’ she says. ‘Farming ostriches, like all the rest. Those big omelets. Who can forget? ... And president of something, governor of somewhere.’

‘Exploration doesn’t seem in your line, Stivelle,’ I say. ‘I don’t like to turn you down ... Maybe there could be another plan for you. I have doubts about you all. It’s the others – I don’t fancy sleeping with them in those little tents....’

‘Well,’ she says. ‘Don’t think you’ll sleep with me.’

‘Oh,’ I say. ‘I’ve been all over. Nearly everywhere, except the Essequibo. I’m discreet....’

‘It’s good,’ she says. ‘Though that is not the word you mean. Try “incomplete”.’

‘You inspire me with your omelet. A menu is a structure, an institution. Like an expedition,’ I say: ‘A code, a legal code – the same thing. It holds – it would hold the five of us wherever we are. We can do anything, manage anything at all. Except the Essequibo – we’re not equipped. We could watch the movie. You’re a fine woman, Stivelle, but you have no useful skills....’

We need more motivation. Something unique, imaginative.

‘You could be governor of the moon, Stivelle,’ I say. ‘Everywhere needs a state, they say, a government.’

‘Is that a good career move, Torsten?’ she asks. ‘Your gift of the impossible? Besides – I have a special sympathy for birds – up on the moon they wouldn't fly. No air to get a grip on. We'd need wear masks – birds would have a problem with their beaks. When our satellite spun off, it would have been full of dinosaurs. And yet, there's been no sign of lives. That book by Galileo – they think it is a forgery.... His ten-cent telescope, it couldn't spot T-Rex.'

'No problem for your ostriches, Stivelle,' I say. 'They'd walk. You'd have a problem with the settlers, though. All that fine equipment, them frivolous and doing leaps. Raising dust. To do most things, you need some air – just to make the laws, to swear in cops....'

'Mostly,' Stivelle says. 'Settlers bring a lot of cows. Up there – there is no grass. We shouldn't be surprised – they say the past is full of oddities, but you should be prepared for futures even more replete with things amazing, not anticipated ... though, I believe there is a song about the moon and cows – I never went to nursery school, I never learned it....'

We're at an impasse. We stare at one another, and we laugh. I never went to nursery school – I say, 'The moon is like Brazil will be. I went there, actually saw the cows....'

'Enough!' says Stivelle. 'Enough of these airless grassless places. Godless and graceless. I see a palace, all in tiers, like the Potala, with figures like the couples on a wedding cake on every tier – only of course, there is no wedding, and the dance is Texmex, spiced with gongs and cymbals....'

'The air is thin there, and there's not much grass,' I say, 'Even if the place existed still....'

'Well, you bastard,' Stivelle says, changing register, flexing up. 'If you want a crumb of truth, sweet as Guyanan chocolate – you must realise: I tell lies, I steal money. It took me years to learn, and you won't trust me, but you'll give me chance after chance, and the reconciliation and forgiveness – it will make us both feel so good, so very good. And I forgive you, Torsten. Ignorance has no fault. No one is responsible for everything. Many a mickle ... but no one knows what mickles are, and most things took place long ago, we never heard about them and most things will take place long after we are dead.'

'You've read a heap of philosophy, Stivelle, that, I can see,' I tell her. 'The others thought they didn't need it, just make it up as life goes on – like the river changes aspect, changes fauna, colour, stretches of mud, dead trees, of chemicals, *morie* of fish and creatures like the dolphin ... that ingratiating grin! ... quite unavailing....

'We'll have time to be together, Stivelle: an abundance. Too much.

'I can see you're used to being close to luxury. And power....'

'Not just close, Torsten,' she says. 'I had those round my neck and arms, and in my navel, in a pyramid upon my head, my sandals, studded in the club in my left hand.'

I say, 'I never saw the picture, Stivelle.'

'If you're a philosopher,' she says, 'you must have subjects. Like a monarch. Like a monarch butterfly the birds won't eat, because you're poison.'

'Oh, these are old tales, Stivelle,' I say, feeling embarrassed by the rush of reminiscence and regret. 'Behaviour, contemplation – if it's not for money coming in, it's to avoid paying out. It comes to much the same.'

'You pick at the past and its geography as if they're strawberries on a buffet,' Stivelle says. 'You're a reactionary.

Partition? Remember separate development? Whips and walls, that's what you promise. Be careful what you fantasise. Your cash and your philosophies – the wealth, the sugared words – all slavery, Torsten. That's where it comes from. How we talk and what we know – all borne on our black backs. You're supposed to know.'

'We choose our times, and our complicities,' I say. 'Slaves made our system You'd start further back, is all. Much further. Other systems: slaves. Still further.... When it's all lawless, inchoate. No one had theorised – and everything's in flux. Creation just new-born and helpless, without laws: before the species organised itself, invented cheap labour, and suffering began. Enslavement's our characteristic, Stivelle, deep in our nature. First slaves then empires – universal slaveries. I can't escape it, but all I talk about's escape. I'm back to "understand the world". I don't think I – or you – will change it.

'If we were very young, we'd be in a gang, perhaps. To terrorise....'

'If we were very young, we'd run a gang....' she says.

'But not die young,' I say.

'Oh, I died young,' Stivelle says. 'It's why I don't care now. I'd robbed banks and been a Bolshevik, and not survived. I am not trustworthy. Perhaps I did all that and beat the rap, survived anonymous.

'Explorers – they lie too, Torsten. Say they climbed, or trudged. It mostly isn't true. To know something remote, you'd ask the locals: if you're keen. Mostly, those who know, invent. We're on a globe – you must return to where you started from if you go straight. Mountains have tops, rivers begin – it's reasonable. Reason – an excess of it leads you from the real and into the obscure. Lies need be reasonable, very, if they're to be believed.'

'The others?' I ask. 'What's to be done? Cyril's an intellectual. That's easy – they don't discover anything, useless to have them trekking up a river to a source. Eternal returns: that is their trade. Finding a thread. It's dull; and then – the rhetoric, the final boast, the goodnight kiss ... the few who say they are philosophers still, have made a papacy with many popes, declaiming from their balcony ... all platitudes. Uplift for believers.

'Believe me, it's their trade. Leave him, he'll do no harm.

'Now – Leos: he's a sailor from a country without sea. Those guys – are ocean truckers. Neither culture nor civilisation – millions of them moving round, not loved, and not resented. Bearers of orders to be filled, delivered, but not by them. He's taken the first step, left family and village, and he roams. It's all the same to him, a life of travel without landfalls .... he thinks he bears the knowledge from his rural friends. It may be so. He knows what everybody he knows, knows: it isn't much.'

'Lucien believes we all know everything, the visible and not,' Stivelle says. 'Each brain's designed to hold it all – equations, mysteries and Proust. It's almost all unused. Deserted palace in the snow: white interiors, the chairs covered in dusty sheets, long corridors and hurrying rats, Torsten ... unless ...' she falters. 'There really isn't much at all. What a disaster! All we've puzzled over – turns out quite simple, two words; and we know, have always known, the everything, the obvious. The mist of ignorance is clouds, they're there to shield us from the burning sun. That sun is

God, the wrathful, the fire where all ends up. And when He dies, we'll all have long before been frizzled up. It's in the book ... you've done all that at school, and chose thereafter to ignore the truth....'

'We don't agree, Stivelle' I say.

I'm not at ease with chaos theorists, like she is, but I've no response. 'So, what do you do, Stivelle? Why are you bound to be my partner, traveller on this little blob, circling in its gritty void...?'

'Oh,' she says, self-deprecating. 'I write Qur'ans. For a small fee, I'll do other holy books; profane ones too. Brought up to date, made to look live. And even feisty. It's like paleontology – you have the skeleton, you plaster on the flesh, give it a diet, then you find the vital spring, instal the soul – and off it roams....'

'Not yet, Stivelle,' I say. 'That was another movie – we're surrounded by a screen, with divas, but they're dying out, the flicks. They take up too much cash, they're dinosaurs who eat your figs, your fig tree.... Now, you can make stories from your house and send them out for free.... Besides, those new Qur'ans – you risk, my dear. Creation has its bounds, its frontiers to respect.... Nothing is innocent, they say: even your ignorance becomes a threat....'

'I am an artist,' Stivelle says. 'Respect me for it! Rob me, stone me – but respect my art!'

'It's true,' I say. 'My trip up-river was to be a journey of discovery. But some discoveries – it's better not insist. Some novelty is good for you, some's not. I hid the purpose of our search, but as a minimum, required from all of you – an epistemology....'

'Oh Torsten!' Stivelle laughs. 'No one does that now – it's sterile, and who cares? Be flexible, like me! Don't be a Cyril – invent! Time bears us all somewhere – onward, and upward! Or just along.... And two of us? It's tough. Exploring needs a team. We couldn't heft the prirogue over massive falls, or cook a turkey-bird on two green sticks....

'And so you've set it up – the usual fudge. "Everything" is off. We all failed the test, not knowing what it was.'

I don't tell her my intent. Maybe that's impossible, until it's realised.

*

'I value loyalty,' I say, 'but naturally, not to me: I've nothing to be loyal to. We can forget Cyril. He is loyal by nature. The other two – we drop them, and we say "it's not about the river. It's about knowledge – the river's not about knowing anything at all. The answer's in the movie." Will it be made, and made by us? That doesn't interest you, not a bit.'

'That's honesty,' Stivelle says. 'Not loyalty. You find honesty in the sausage shop.'

We laugh. It's true. 'Leos,' I begin.

'You know what they say,' she says. 'Czechs don't fight.'

'The Russians said that,' I say. 'It's not always so.'

'The Russians have always fought,' she says. 'That's the difference. Forget Leos. That leaves Lucien.'

'He thinks we know it all already – everything is confirmation of a detail,' I say. 'Knowing and comprehending seem the same. "This molecule cures that disease. Well! Who would have thought it. Always obvious, and always so....” He’ll never be impressed.’

‘Lucien knows it’s not about the river, its sad destiny,’ she says. ‘It’s all about the movie you don’t want to make; the report, denunciation. Everybody knows already, not just Lucien. Anyone with eyes can see how it’s all ending – the battle for survival means we eat up all the food, and then we’re finished. Or we do it slowly, and we farm, and it goes on and on. Like dinosaurs. They never made it to the moon, Torsten. We did; there’s nothing there you wouldn’t find in Africa, and you’d steal it.... Everybody’s looking while you loot; who cares?’

‘His gun?’ I ask. ‘What was his crime? To be a victim of an accident?’

‘He wanted to kill somebody. His old gun exploded. That is all,’ she says. ‘The law ... at the end, it always sums things up.’

‘I’m on edge, Stivelle,’ I say: ‘You are a risky type. Risk seems to drive you. And in the wake – the smell of death.’

‘Going in the jungle, Torsten,’ she says, laughing hard. ‘It’s a risk. And people everywhere – they go to see the bull, the dogs, the boxers and the cars. Is it the risk they watch, or death they hope for and expect? You can’t separate things to please yourself. Escape or smash – it can’t be planned. You can’t keep thinking twice before.’

‘I want something definitive, Stivelle,’ I say. ‘Risk and chance – that muddies it before the contests start. People in my life – they come, they go, they chatter and they lounge ... then all is swept away, as if an act has ended, no one sang the aria, still less performed the final joust.... Another cast comes on, starts performing quite a different opera, the players change their instruments, the pianist walks the dog, it's cha-cha time and then once more it's not.... And you know your act will come and go as well, if you don't work it differently, which no one ever has....'

'Oh,' she says. 'I want something big. You have to bring the bigness to it, though – it doesn't just invent itself.'

'You're younger than me, Stivelle,' I say. 'You're all beautiful, where you come from, but you ... you … you rock, my dear!'

'I love you Torsten,' Stivelle says. 'There. You thought people didn't say that now. I'm primitive. Do you believe me? Is it invention, to get money, a platform? Let's be honest. Are you lovable? Or do you know you aren't? Know yourself and all your deeds and thoughts? Can I love your blur and blot?

'Think of your belief, the horrors incysted in it. Don't you know – leaving people to themselves, their ignorance, good will – it opens them to exploitation, enslavement and the rest ... And don't you know too, you intervene with people and – it opens them to exploitation, enslavement and the rest.... Is my love for you invention, do you think? Most things are inventions – the radio, the polygraph, the cluster bomb....'

'I'm very careful with my thoughts, Stivelle,' I say. 'I know you are. There's nothing light in you.'

'If you could paint,' she says. 'I'd be your model a hundred years ago, and make you big. Make you create. But you don't create, not ever. You peer, Torsten The peering style – is yours! You can't paint anyway, and I would spit on all that sitting still.'

DISENCHANTMENT

'We've talked,' I say. 'And it's been long and cordial. And I don't know anything you know. It's good, I'd say. It's as if you'd forgotten everything – if you had family, what's your island, your cat's name....'

'It was a canary,' says Stivelle. 'I had many, forgotten all their names.'

'The other three from the bar will take it bad, that I won't call them,' I say.

'Of course,' she says. 'You asked them what they know, and how. They told you everything, but you gave nothing of yourself. They're humiliated. They'll always hate you. Be puzzled too.'

'I don't know many things,' I say. 'I contrive mosaics, hoping they spell out mosaic law. The little pieces – they accumulate. Keep the bus tickets. Collect them all, the scraps, put them together, make a picture. There's no way of knowing what style, what format, if it's precise, where it comes from, what it represents. It coheres, that's all. A frame contains it.'

'It's a Byzantine argument,' Stivelle says. 'But we love Byzantium. All peoples lived there happily, it grew small, grew tiny, then they opened the back door, in came the Osmanlis – and the huge souk that they set up the first month was marvellous, all China, all Sogdia, all India, all Syria ... all Iran.'

*

'This picture, Torsten,' Stivelle asks. 'Where do you keep it? In your head? And can I see it.'

'Oh, the brain?' I ask. 'That's just the crate I keep things in. The pictures hang upon the walls. Some you can recognise, and some are swirls, and some are windows – just blank panes.... The landscape is outside, sometimes it's clouds....'

'How do brains tell us how to live?' she asks. 'It doesn't seem to fit at all. That geloid structure – seems it's crucial, but instead – it isn't relevant to anything. We most of us have legs, and left legs too – they are similar, though some are bowed, and some are not. So what?'

'That's why I bring the river in,' I say. She's not convinced. 'It's big enough to be a metaphor, and unexplored – so it could serve as anything at all. Future and past, decline and sprout.'

'You could grow rice,' she says. 'And sell it, eat it, and that way you wouldn't need beg Hari for some cash.'

'That's right,' I say. 'There is no cash. It's spent, it's stolen. It won't come back.'

'Do you want to inform?' she asks. 'To lead? Watch other people, attach yourself to them?'

'Yes,' I say. 'Some of that. I'd ask – why do we search, go places? Find out what we can think are novel things? Although there's risk and boredom, it's always us, ourselves, pilot and engine, seeking disappointments, confirmation, and amazements. Amusements.'

*

Lucien says, 'I speak with tongues – my own, and Cyril's and Leos's. They know I persist, I use all means. I got my wounds from seeking a redress. I was not respected. This lad – he was my lover. Or better – I was his. I loved. No. I lent him pride, my pride. He did not appreciate. He didn't ask me "Was it a gift? A loan?"'

I'm afraid of Lucien's guns. One is accounted for. Maybe he has more, and more resentments.

'I'll handle Lucien,' says Stivelle.

'I'm the principal, Stivelle,' I say, very quietly.

'You are air, Torsten,' she says. 'You have no consistency, no trade.'

'What do you know?' I ask.

'I don't need to know anything,' she says. 'I'm a seductress. Sex doesn't enter. I lead you strictly by the nose.'

Lucien breaks in, 'I'm blind. When we reach the source, will you be sure to put me in the pic? It makes no difference to you, but any difference to me's immense.'

'Of course you'd be put in,' I say. 'Expeditions leave the drivers and the carriers in a separate group – only the experts get a credit. You, Lucien – you'd be our expert in knowing and not seeing. Qualified in blindness and its puzzles....'

'You have an interesting face, Lucien,' says Stivelle. 'What a pity you can't see it....'

'No one can see their face,' says Lucien. 'And I saved my honour too.... No one's seen that, not ever.'

'Or was it anger, Lucien?' I ask. 'A raptus, impulse?'

'Yes,' Lucien says. 'Why not? I am profound. You never reach the bottom of my motivations.... It's similar to your search, Torsten, except there is no glory and no cash, no record and no praise.'

'Mine's not a search where you find something that isn't where you look,' I say. 'And in your case – you cannot look. What's to be found – you can find it by sitting in your chair.'

'We can't be satisfied,' says Lucien. 'You wanted to recruit us, and were devious. Where do we go? Why?'

*

'You're not much use,' Stivelle says. 'As a recruiter. You're more usually recruited yourself. So far you've discarded half of those you interviewed – and here they come again! What's most promising is a blind man and a seductress. It's a joke – and are you the jester? A jester needs a Prince, someone to amuse and punish him, to show a joke is serious. You know the structures are all there; have been since I came out of Africa, long after you had left. Now – all we can do is see which ones still stand. You're right – a river might be one of them. But – it's quite marginal. Rivers will dry up, never reach the sea. They'll make a lake, and then one night – it too will disappear. We want to be progressive, and rebellious – but you've seen, we are reactionary. We long for how it should have been and never was, will never be. And yet, and yet – best believe that no one knows and no one interferes.

'We want what others more ignoble have already had, gobbled down, despoiled, polluted.... Used, damaged, goods, high prices.

'We want for us what they thought was the good life. They had it. So, despite everything, do we believe we shall?' she asks.

'If it comes, we shall be happy, those of us who want,' I say. 'Anyway, you read those antique texts. It takes a lifetime to read just one. Mostly, we don't bother. It's not worth a life, we think, even if we give it ours....'

'Copying – it makes you understand. It helps. It is the same for me,' she says. 'I go to the root, what we are: on two legs. A common animal.'

'But, you want understanding. Something that you can have, and then ignore,' I say.

'I want assimilation. Ingestion of the word. I'm tired of reading and misunderstanding – I want to be the word made flesh – my flesh. Maybe only then can I be heterodox,' she says. 'Or disbelieve, knowing profoundly what I don't believe. It works for Descartes and for Tarski too....' She laughs.

I laugh. 'It seems perverse,' I say. 'Although I understand. It's me, I guess – except I don't deal with books. I've drifted towards rivers – that are made of sentences and plots and pararaphs, changes of sense and register: the currents, eddies. Colours. Smells.... Impersonalities.'

'Yes,' she says. 'That's life, the lesson, but,' and she turns away, 'it's short, too short to have you make a difference, or to pass one on. And – it doesn't cheer! As with your river – you start at one end, and reach the other – the significance would lie in going back, over and over, deeper, measuring.... You never can. You never do.'

'I'm unveiling the metaphor,' I say. 'And find it's just a metaphor. I believed it was a river! I'm understanding life – I don't know what to do with it. Not with life, nor understanding either. I'm depressed. It's the river's fault....'

'Metaphors don't wear veils. Veils are everything,' she says. 'They protect you, but they show you're weak. Yes or no – do we pry into the Essequibo?'

'We should explore this fucking river,' I say. 'Maybe there will be a clue.'

'Cyril thinks we ought not go,' she says. 'The first people to go somewhere – they're like a line of ants. There is a line of them, a ramp, rampage: not a first explorer, who ends the tale, finds the unknown, the magic golden men. Could there be a number one, a first ant? What matters is the number – what they eat, carry away, obscure with thousands of their presences. It's a new history, the transforming throng. Those ants, in their city-hill – do they think of something more than being ants? Reproducing exactly what they are?

'Lucien was fortunate – he didn't start a line of murders: he began a set of accidents; that's quite harmless, happens all the time.'

'All the same, he'll go,' I say. 'And not by accident.'

'A thing turns out to be another thing,' she says. 'Lucien found that out! Vengeance, honour, punishment – are they the same? He didn't think – he suffered! Revelation's blinding. You think, "just a flash in the pan"! Instead, you over-egged, you over-powdered, blew up your weapon, and you get two barrel-loads of pain.

'The lesson is, there can't be lessons. As you know – I think there is no past, it all starts over in this instant....

'And Leos – says he knows these rural scenes, knows how to talk to people, understands the fears.... He'll reassure the people that we meet – we'll come, and go, taking our rubbish with us in big sacks....'

'It's nonsense. Nothing's up to Leos,' I say. 'Nature means fear – no one can give you reassurance – not gods nor devils: they're always lurking, very close. Besides, the people shouldn't interest us. They'll have a story; valued things they'll want to have protected. They'd know we won't leave pristine what we have found. We'd come to light dark places, and people who live in them, made them, want them dark.

'Our intentions are impeccable. It doesn't mean a thing. I realise – curiosity breaks the crocks, unavoidably, and they cannot be repaired. Am I a breaker? I'm not sure. Probably....'

'Only us four answered to the ad,' she says. 'Take it as you will.'

'Everybody answered – you four represent all the responses there can be,' I say.

That isn't true. Killers, fugitives.... people who want a place to live ... they would explore, seek a home.

There's lots of them. Hard cases – everywhere, abundantly. I don't want them with me.

It could be any one of us.

INSTEAD, THE MOVIE

We don't go, of course. Think for a moment: it would be unthinkable. Knowledge – it tells us we can't know all we want. Stivelle and me – we're not ready to go paddling. Still less a portage. Think again: some more.

The five of us ... instead, we watch the movie. The makers, the creators, to give us the movie, they had stormed into the garden, with coils of cable, generators: lessons too. Expelled those they didn't trust. They exposed the people who'd been there for almost ever, gave them the taste: strange fruits; the pomegranate. They judged, they tempted.

Men and women on the moon, they were shown the earth, given a document. They'd always known everything, known the moon was small, much smaller than the world.

Had they? It's what Lucien says.

We'll never know.

They were opened up like oysters.

*

'We have a relationship, Torsten,' Stivelle says. 'We understand what we both mean. I've work to do upon myself – whatever that may bring. But you, Torsten – without a job, a family, a place – you're a figure found in operas. You sing, but you've no background. We'd hate to be with you stuck in an elevator. Why are you here? What do you accomplish?'

'I'll tell you when we have to run,' I say. 'Then you should see. We are not innocent. We are not guilty. You've been banned, driven out your country, and on a list. Nowhere to go back to. I have vendetta, hung on Manlio. There's trouble for me if he escapes. Or if he stays inside.

'Lucien – put too much powder in his weapon – it's clear he'll maybe try again on someone else.... He has shown his hand. That leaves Leos: naive and dealing....'

'It's the Germans,' Stivelle says. 'To get away from them, Czechs like Leos have to go to sea, and then they don't know what to do. Seek greatness? Cry in your bunk – remembering the geese, the hips and haws, the dance....

'That's what you ought to do, Torsten. You're nature's Czech.'

*

A bunch of policemen, and a line of soldiers. The police have many different arms – sticks and stones: to winkle out an eye, hit to the head; the manual says you use your night-stick to break the collarbone, incapacitate – but who remembers that? Go for the brain! It works! Greek fire in canisters – use if it rains.... Make order – it's quite indispensable. We need and fear them, the police. If we were better, we would like them more, perhaps. There's a price. You pay.

The soldiers are quite different. Soldiers: each has a gun: they are at ease, or all attention, when their single officer says. A queen, she's called, with wings, who flies.

Think ants, not bees!

Bees specialise, they do different tasks, discriminate through gender – each created for her job, or just to lounge around and die. Their society – is ordered, you'd not say it was so complex, unless you're Mandeville or Maeterlinck. They dance! They improvise: that old soldier, Virgil, observed – 'his helmet now a nest for bees'. Honey and survival: that's it! The bees instruct us, more than the ants? It's the honey gives them visibility, significance and usefulness. They're fun: can go extinct. They will. Ants, though – will inherit the earth. A presence not so gratifying. They fascinate, and mostly they aren't fun. It takes hard work, being ants.

Killer bees and soldier ants – the copy-cats! Robots on the march.

Maybe we humans have diversified too much, and uselessly. Neither honey nor survival attract us as goals for life. We think we're more complicated. What's our legacy, our product? What's the speciality? Puzzles? Riddlemerees? Beggar-my-neighbour? The shell game? Equations, prayers?

Our nests: the poorest tin-towns have the brightest colours, feisty music, more life, more death.

*

'"The days were not far off when nothing would save one except chance,"' I say. 'Stivelle – take note. Hope Abandoned – makes you feel better. Whatever you had in mind that got you banned – you're now in with the rest of us. No 'letters of repentance to the newspapers' – nothing at all will help. Join in the crowd – you might be gassed, or have an eye pinged out, a jaw knocked slant for ever – or, you might reach your goal....

The pawn made queen. All is lost, except ideals, every card been played except the last one, face down before you.... Your ace in the hole, the hole that's the last for all of us.'

'Keep fishing, Torsten,' Stivelle says. 'My story is banal – a life of prick and sting, getting under hides, scales and skins. You provoke, they nip; you bite, they swipe. You wonder how you went so long. Don't try to ride on me, my friend! – be sure, if I find a place to go, I shan't kneel down and have you ride.'

'Letters,' I say. 'Mail. That's where Leos went astray. Maybe it's not specialisation that's at fault – it's refinement. Chew the leaves – but don't refine the coca. It went bad for Leos. He'd always struggled for that job: the postman. Opening up the world. He delivered everything, to everyone. Too much.'

'They say it was the human sacrifice – did for the Incas,' says Stivelle. 'Not the coca. They had three thousand varieties of potato. That's an obsession, Torsten.... They had pony express as well.'

'I have my doubts,' I say. 'About accounts of why all civilisations fell. They had an answer, but their good order, their perfection, fell foul of the impermanence of everything. Nothing is made to last, Stivelle. What saddens me's their heritage. What they left, after the wars, the sicknesses, the boredom, rivalries – are the deserts of the world. They make us wail, despair. These places, once green and impenetrable, were cleared and harrowed ... the trees burnt to made a stucco, or a pyre. The coronation inaugurates the building of the pyramid which uses labour of a thousand years.

'If only – they'd just left the stories: the knotted strings that tell a tale, the landing strips for Martians, the sun's secret life.... Forget the palaces, the desolations. Leave a puzzle. Thousands of holes – a testament, a novel or a star-map? A word's supposed to make a picture or a sound – it doesn't, obviously ... so why not holes? Holes could constitute language, a vocabulary – except....'

'Except we don't know what it means,' says Stivelle. 'Not in the slightest. They could be an abacus. Holes in the sand ... like a literal prick-text, a massive braille? Pianola rolls adapted for your feet?

'Those teeming people – compassionate, and cruel enough to know what life could be for those about to lose it. Was there a secret? Death as a door: had they opened it, gone through, come back?'

'Words are a veil,' I say. '*The* veil. Those holes: would they make a story? Would it amuse, illuminate? Or was it their all: their life, their brain? Did they leave words we cannot understand, that hide what we can't see?'

'It's too repetitive,' Stivelle says. 'Holes, a metre deep! Life is a tale. What isn't? We need a halt, hiatus: something that proceeds unchanging. A tale without familiarity, conclusions. I think of the falls on the Essequibo; I use them to send me off to sleep.'

'We all do that,' I say. 'And see the otters play behind the curtain, wait for the fish to fall into their timetable.'

I feel the tears press. Ridiculous. Being an otter? – not my ambition, ever. And to say you watch them, miss them – it can't be!

CYRIL

'I've learnt,' he says. 'Not to confess. Not to expose. It does nothing for you – indeed, it's a pain. Why gratify another? Someone you wouldn't know?

'We five started out as explorers. Now – our stories have come out, and we're a band of fugitives and chancers. The unfortunate, the ineffective. I'm out of place among you. I can't say I'm innocent.... I'm not guilty, though.

'In medical school – the first day was epiphany. Hundreds of us, waiting, studying for admission to the bourgeoisie. What do you have to do? In these rural lands, the doctors are the angels of enlightenment, those who know everything your granpa has forgot, the *farmaka,* the cures for life. The means: dissection – that's what intellectuals do, that makes them so unpopular. They cut you up, your argument. But here a pack....

'Of animals. Little animals – on every desk, a tiny one pinned out, to be cut up, despatched illegible – to the incinerator. I looked round – everyone was slicing, or pondering where to start. A massacre, a mutilation. What you do to enemies – with a machete, you cut off the spigot, then the feet, the legs and arms, and carve. But these small creatures, famous for their scuttering....

'I knew then I was not a humanist. I was part of something larger – maybe a river and its banks.

That night, someone in my dormitory played a sex game with himelf, got aphasia, choked and died. Would he too be served up on our desks, a sliver each? Maybe a chief would say – 'Everybody – try a poem ... an epitaph! The guy's a nobody. Write poetry upon his bones.'

'And so – I left. There was nothing else that I could do. Would I become a priest? A politician? Replace cruelty with lies? Not a chance.

'I've been an excellent doctor. I read the mags in waiting rooms – they tell you everything: – what diseases – as they say – "rampage". More supplicants died than recovered. Better than that – no one, for sure no god – can do.'

'Sex, I knew was risky, even by yourself. Unthinkable with others.'

He takes a black stump, once a cigar, a *toscana,* from a leather case, beautifully tooled, you'd want to study it.... You smell his cloud, his cloud of smoke, shortening the lives around.

'That's it?' asks Stivelle. 'You make up the set, Cyril. Exploring to escape.We are a band of people set on paths we must run crouching on. In silence and by night....'

'Cyril,' I say. 'Being a fake is neutral: so, tell. Did your patients die? Because of you?'

'Because?' he asks. 'Do you want an answer from philosophy? Causality's a knotty beast. Let's stay with common sense for now. Oh yes: they die, already, or to come. Not because of me. Because they were sick. I understand those signs – in those there is no mystery, the future's absolutely clear.'

'Your motivation, then?' Stivelle asks. 'Coming here, unqualified. To reach the source, or watch the lives flung out to sea ... after they have reached the delta?'

'Nothing of that,' he says. 'The gold.... It must be everywhere, underfoot, in these awful countries – nature hides it, best as it can, and if you want it, you must go down to hell.' He pauses. 'And then spread hell like a fever, everywhere.'

'You've done well,' says Stivelle. 'You became an intellectual after all, and did exactly what the intellectuals do. Dissect, renounce, deny. Commit, retreat. What was lacking, possibly, was a stipend. An abode. A desk. You tried a cure for life, when death already had its fingers on your heart and twiddling in your brain. All you felt was genuine. Your patients were yourself, dead guinea-pigs pinned out....'

'Oh,' Cyril says. 'That's what they say: "You failed, but that's success!" That's all hohum, a faddle fiddled. But anyway – you're right, what lacked all my life was – recognition, which anyone can estimate in gold.'

'The other two,' I say, much disturbed. 'Lucien, Leos, want retribution, promise restitution. Above all, if there is another path, they'd like to try it. You don't believe there are alternatives. Take Stivelle: – did you want justice?' I ask her.

'No,' she says. 'I wanted power. With power – maybe I'd have handed out some justice. Don't confuse the game.'

'Well,' I say, disappointed, not surprised. 'What do the four adventurers want? For you, Stivelle, it's just an interlude, a challenge, time to pass. But for Leos, Lucien and Cyril – was it life they sought? Hung for ever over the falls – there's clouds. On those – maybe you can see there's perched a figure: divine? Semi? Despised, degraded? Through the mist, it's hard to make it out. Maybe my team would want a better vantage point? A view from the stalls, perhaps: stalls at the opera or the races, for them, it would be the same.'

'Gold,' says Stivelle. 'The team, they wanted gold. They scented it. It's on the maps. Gold exchanges easily for anything. It must be hidden all around, or guys would not be here, to dig and suffer. Exploit, be skinned, be suffocated....'

'This moralism, Stivelle,' I say. 'Forget it. It does not go well with everything we two have said, and shared.'

'If we had gone,' she says, 'we were well prepared. Cyril for the surgery. Leos – plants, herbs and entertainment. Lucien – the military arm and – let's say: "intelligence". And I'd do all the rest. You, Torsten, would talk to indigenes – explain to them what you can't tell us – why you take us on. How you hope to bring them innocence – yours, and add it to what you think is theirs. Delusions, naturally. You're in science and the spectacle – neither of those cares. We don't wish to explore, but just be paid excessively. And when we make discoveries, we're bound to keep them to ourselves, so we can go back and profit from them other times....'

'Yes, Stivelle,' I say. 'Exactly. You are those who ought to go: and why we won't. And – I'm different, because I had the plan! I shall not go....'

NEW PROJECTS

'I'll miss the river jaunt,' Stivelle says. 'But there's much more that we can do – finance, fighting – medicating, saving the species. All is open to us.'

'Yes,' says Cyril. 'But those lizards – green and blue, with their red air-sacs – the tiny wings that presage evolutions bold – to see them gliding, leaping, catching the light like scimitars.... I should have told their tales....'

'And there's the moon,' says Lucien. 'Over in Guyane, the country has been destroyed ... an immense pad for rockets going to the stars. But here – if you could make a ladder – when the moon comes very near, and red – you could climb up, and maybe, maybe, with a stick, a crook – you'd snag it, not to pull it down, but pull yourself up to it – frolic in its red sand; a continent.... Being blind, the universe is close, snug in my head, accessible, a crystal drop. And the dance! You need that to get you in the mood....'

'The figure on the clouds?' asks Stivelle, with some sarcasm. 'Maybe he was a moonman, maybe slightly stoned, slipped off the moon when he tried to clamber back, on to a cloud and there remains....'

'You laugh,' says Leos, laughing too. 'You haven't seen the half of what a normal postie sees on his first day, first round, before he parcels out his laughing-dust.... Centuries ago, trips by means of ladder or balloon, from Prague to moon – were frequent: much enjoyed. An escape – to music grannie hummed. It's true – there's nothing there, no dance halls, no beer-garden, nothing, nothing: absolutely zilch at all....

'But when these visits were no more – we fell into confusion. Read the literature, Hasek, Kafka.... When you can no longer leave, fly, or ramp up, to the heavens – there's confusion, a terrible, disorienting sprawl upon the earth. If the moon is inaccessible – so's all the rest. The universe becomes a wormhole, a what-the-butler-saw – a bagatelle, a desolation for quixotic vagabondage ... a trip.

'I'm unlettered, that is clear. But remember – our voyaging, without a smoke or snort – gave us our home, our roots. Roots of the moon – that's where we start.

'The moon, my friends! Look where reason led a country, *la Guyane*; ravaged to blast off rockets! A vast launching pad! Bangers! A ladder, or a coach and pair – it's quite enough. So many, like me, forced to take the sailor's way – we used to sail by stars and moons, the tides responded – but no more.... Some guy sits before his screen, and steers. Boat, rocket – they're the same. Imagine! That's it! That's all!'

'Everything is banal, everything is predictable,' says Lucien. 'In that, I'm with Leos. Whether you climb up to it, or dredge for it in the bottom of the well, the moon's a great temptation – it changes colour like a ripening fruit, it comes close, it winks, it disappears – over and over. It's like the ancient metaphor – every life's a river, every river's life.... Machado said it once again in poetry. In jail, we heard it was the Madre de Dios, a *foco* for guerillas. That is the way, we said. The only answer to eternal repetition is the act: the action.... Propaganda by the deed. The fall of the market-spectacle economy. "We know the battlefield." We're in it.

Everybody looks for action, something unexpected, decisive.... "The foot that stamps on the ants' nest will be an ant's foot...."'

'I don't see that, Lucien,' says Stivelle.

'That's the point,' says Lucien. 'I don't see anything at all. The act! I don't see, can't do – though I remember everything. *On s'engage...!*'

*

'I have a plan,' Stivelle says. 'Forget the moon. Nothing to do with rivers. And it's not a metaphor.'

*

'We four, we answered the ad,' says Stivelle. 'The only ones: – you might have expected millions. Not so. It must mean we're trustworthy and believed. Loyal to you, Torsten, over all other other causes, countries, and their flags....

'We're not up to exploring the river. That's good – for us, for all the indigenes. A hundred years ago, they took people from Guyane, took the celebrated captive Moliko – put them in a human zoo. Racism, supremacy, fascism, death. It's been done: those scoundrels! Done, exposed, and done again. Another name is given, but the same exercise repeats – variations on the theme.... Don't pretend to weep – you're a kind of crocodile, but your tears – they don't impress.

'We are a team, though. Instead of many projects, we'll be logical, put them into one. We'll bring the wretched of the earth some food, and add some capital. That's what you need when you are in distress – the cash. We'll set the broken limbs, improvise a puppet show, hand out some spliffs – and Lucien will organise defence. He'll shoot at sight, be the security. That's what you need, along with cash. Everything is known about the destitutes – we'll be the ones that can resolve it all.'

'I put the ad,' I say. 'So – what's next for me?'

'The cash, Torsten,' she says. 'You give the cash.'

'Oh, the unknown god?' I say. 'He isn't me, and I don't believe in Him. Maybe the little figure on the cloud ... can pee down gold....'

Remember what Hari said. There's nothing, nothing left, he doesn't trust me, is indifferent. If there was some resource, he'd have questioned me, seen if I'm a serious type. Nothing, instead. There's no resource, we spent it all.

*

'Lucien,' I say, 'you've known confinement. I imagine it is black inside your eyes, and time unattainable, outside, without the life-world....'

'Not black,' he says. 'It's colourless. Emotions every day. The noise is good; that shows it's light, and you begin each day the rote – anxiety, depression, then there's melancholy; touching familiar things, a flash of a euphoria beyond reason, too intense to be enjoyable, then gone for ever, unreachable – you're in a well, no water, but you're never thirsty. A plan – intense and intricate, but you're not in it, it's all round you. It won't end, because there's nothing left, nowhere to be, nothing: and no one round to give you nothing.'

'There must be....' I begin. I don't know what....

'Afterwards, I thought I would have fought,' he goes on, not turning his face to me. 'A war. I'd have fought the war the Bosniaks did. Freedom, subjection, freedom – a promise, then confinement, imprisonment. That's the story, the history. Being, not being. I recognise all that, and I'd have fought, never compromised, never surrendered. I thought afterwards I'd really fought that war. Imagine it – a blind man fighting: even an army of blind men.... The other side would be terrified!'

'It's all strange to me,' I say. 'All I wanted was to find a starting place, to see the animals doing what they have to do – at least, the herbivores, the granivores. To listen to the rush of water.

'That war, Lucien, the one that you weren't in – I can't imagine being in it, wondering where was the start, and would it end. Is it a river, with a terminus – or a moon, always enduring?'

'Oh,' says Lucien. 'I'm not like you. I'm a good soldier. I fight for myself, to keep alive, to win. You – are the opposite. No wonder they all dropped you. No one cares. You did nothing that was brave. They all got tired of you. You admired the warriors, admired your Elodie – she was frightened, but you'd not done anything to frighten, and yet you too were were terrified.'

'I thought her way was decisive, Lucien,' I say. 'Then it seemed a useless pedagogy. A battle for justice, always too late.

'Punishment. Punish the past. It must be done, it's never finished. It's an unsatisfying, inadequate response. It should correct the future, and forewarn. It never does. Like making revolution, and you find you're constrained to betray it all, cut off the dullards' and the traitors' heads, and all that's maybe left is a few guys – immovable, in what they gave in faith, in loyalty, right at the start: unmovable. Nostalgic for a future that will never be attained.'

'You gave nothing, Torsten, as there's nothing you could give,' says Lucien. 'You thought you'd be clean and pure, find out all about the river, because you couldn't harm it. Then – you'd go away, do something else. Thought it would be easy.'

And he laughs, we laugh.

*

'We can't be many things,' says Stivelle, 'but there is one thing ... and we'll be paid for it. We'll set up as a group – of mediators. We understand all claims, all weaknesses. They're us. We've experienced all provocations. We'll put an ad – "We take any case, at any level. Solutions definitive, without recourse to law, to arms, invasions."'

And that we do.

*

It works.

It's boring. We are rich, successful.

It's unbearable. People – not us! – are dull. They're full of goodwill and spite. Unless you have spies and an army, all settlements go back to what there was before.

We don't give the money back; we spend it. Maybe that's the same.

'The point is,' says Stivelle. 'We should be on the other side. Disaccord and contestation. Everyone is struggling to survive and reach a top. Mediations – they are softball. We should join the conflicts....'

And we do.

But first, Hari approaches me: I tell him, 'When Odette lost her mind, Hari, you should have followed her – into the trees, the roiling water that has disappeared.... Suffer, Hari! Forget the cash....'

'She didn't lose her mind,' he says. 'She found another one, and copyrighted it. It's genius. Besides, where would we cash-doctors be, if you guys didn't smoke, shoot up, buy tin cars in nursery colours?'

And he laughs, makes 'broom-broom' noises, hugs me, pats me down.

'I have ambitions, Hari, not ready cash,' I say.

I hope he doesn't join us – he's a bully.

Conflict and mediation – they're inseparable.

We'll do both, both at the same time.

*

Hari says, 'You need to watch it, Torsten. Don't believe people you've met by electronic means. Lucien's an addict: no tracks, but he's dependent on *cachase*. It's Brazilian, they don't make it here – so, he shakes like willow-leaves: his bones will smoulder, then they'll burn with everlasting fire....

'Leos – an explorer, yes. Trips to the moon: out through your bedroom window, a lunar guide will take your hand and pull you up, you lunatic...! And Cyril, the prison doctor – shortens sentences, adds full-stops ... a drastic editor!'

'Stivelle deals with personnel,' I say. 'If you want taking on, Hari, lower your crest, and chirp your homage.'

'You might be useful, Torsten,' Hari says. 'But you're all aimless. All's been done, or yet to do. You could be "Guardians of the Forest". But you're not. Only you, Torsten, may find your path, when all is nearly finished, and all's lost....'

*

'Wherever we intend to go,' I tell Stivelle. 'We'll go at once, and not take Hari. He'd steal our victories!'

And off we go. New life!

NEW LIFE

'This has turned out to be an end-game,' I say. 'Saying goodbye, hoping everything will change.'

We sit outside the bar, that's built out, over the water. Here they recruit guys for adventures far away ... it's the depositary where they convalesce when they come back – or, if they've been in jail, or shocked in body, soul, they wait to be recruited once again. And so it all revolves, and some drop out or off, the sprightly barmen change and change, and Cyril takes a turn behind the bar.... It gives him company. His cures and his philosophy depend on it.

The water here – it's not a Ganges, you don't get slid in, dead and blessed. The water's brown: it looks up at the moon and you: it has brown skin, brown eyes, it's just a pond, you see it through the shaky decking where you drink and smoke. Once linking to its river, now, like us, it stands.

*

Hari says, 'We'll rescue Manlio: I'll take a posse. Then you'd better watch it, Torsten,' and he struts. He's wearing red ballooning Turkish trousers, like a pirate chief. It reminds me of Odette – how she liked her women dressing strong, a bit exaggerated. No one stares. I think of Elodie, white-grey, in grey-white clothes, at the window, watching the steep road.

I don't believe the threat. The species-project I locked Manlio in – it cannot fail, there's too much cash invested. It's tough, like training for the astronauts – but they endure. Like them, it's hooked on up and down. Manlio won't accept a liberation, he'll persevere – his uniform will say he's superman....

'I have a world-view, Stivelle,' I say. 'There's an infinity of projects to be done. Maybe it's true – the picture's been there from the start. It all depends on how you sort through what you see, and try to make it have a sense ... and ask what any picture's for. All different sorts – there's maps and canvasses, stuff wrapped, installed – and then there's 'scapes, of land and cities. It's not just personal – those make designs that fit designs the others make. Remember what I said right at the start, it's how you know determines what it is you see – in that bar, "Bar dello Sport", when I had put the ad. We chase our tails.

'For me, it's not just plans and explorations – it's about communicating with you all. Not everybody goes in deep – maybe they're right, it isn't deep at all, it's just immediate, and what you need right now....'

'I'll wait for amnesty,' says Stivelle, not listening. 'Then I'm off, back home. Once you've been fingered, though, it's probable you'll be expelled another time. For sure we'll meet again.'

She smiles, not sad at all. 'Mine's not the life....' she says. 'That finds a plinth. See – Leos and Lucien – they're already lost to you,' and she points. 'They're lucky – they forget.'

The couple sit apart from us, talking close of what risky trade or derring-do might suit.... Lucien, the blind gunman, bringing terror, justice as we're used to it. Blind as a stone.

Leos, bringing the pills that make you big or small, down in the burrow where the clocks run fast....

*

Stivelle's determined, lucid, as she leaves. I'd thought between us two all was inconclusive. I was wrong. She writes 'the end'....

'What you had in mind,' Stivelle says, 'has nothing relevant to what people do today. You're not a showman, you've no cash. Up the river to the forest – it's a cliché. Now, everything is planned, foreseen. Especially the return.

'Anything there's left to be discovered, *you*, Torsten, would want to keep it for yourself. If there's ancestors at the source, they'll be modest, and they'll have the same fear you have. Warriors, slaves – all defenceless. They are your sort, you'll salute them, every one of them ... and then move on. Moving slow – you're a mercenary, a sponge. You drag what you use for feet.

'You realise – there's nothing more, nothing you don't know. That's what you've always said. It's so, that's how we all can function, because we know the next step, and how everything turns out to be.'

'Vain, I know,' I say, 'to think we'd find – not meaning, but something meaningful. A beginning and an end that isn't merely melancholy, but is complete. Life not erased by death.... or negligence, or time expired. Life as it is, and having no alternative, life as it ought to be.'

'Hah! Puffs of air,' she shouts, and laughs quite loud, 'Hallucinations. Indifferent birds. The colibrì – yourself. You didn't need a crew at all!'

She wants me to share her summary, our end. 'You'll invent something, though. I'm sure of that,' she says.

Out she strides, off the deck, leaves me to pay the bills. She shouts back:

'You? Explorer of the flux of life? A joke! You're hoping you will find a point between the past and what will come. And hover there.

'The moment of Creation!'

About the author

John Fraser has lived near Rome since 1980. Previously, he worked in England and Canada.

www.ingramcontent.com/pod-product-compliance
Lightning Source LLC
Chambersburg PA
CBHW020549310726
48979CB00008B/1150/J
9781910301890